PENGUIN PLAYS

BROKEN GLASS

Arthur Miller was born in New York City in 1915 and studied at the University of Michigan. His plays include *All My Sons* (1947), *Death of a Salesman* (1949), *The Crucible* (1953), *A View from the Bridge* and *A Memory of Two Mondays* (1955), *After the Fall* (1963), *Incident at Vichy* (1964), *The Price* (1968), *The Creation of the World and Other Business* (1972), and *The American Clock* (1980). He has also written two novels, *Focus* (1945) and *The Misfits*, which was filmed in 1960, and the text for *In Russia* (1969), *Chinese Encounters* (1979), and *In the Country* (1977), three books of photographs by his wife, Inge Morath. His most recent works are *Salesman in Beijing* (1984), *Danger: Memory! Two Plays* (1987), *Timebends*, a memoir (1988), *The Ride Down Mt. Morgan* (1991), and *The Last Yankee* (1993), both plays. He has twice won the New York Drama Critics Circle Award, and in 1949 he was awarded the Pulitzer Prize.

BY ARTHUR MILLER

DRAMA

The Golden Years
The Man Who Had All the Luck
All My Sons
Death of a Salesman
An Enemy of the People (*adaptation of the play by Ibsen*)
The Crucible
A View from the Bridge
After the Fall
Incident at Vichy
The Price
The American Clock
The Creation of the World and Other Business
The Archbishop's Ceiling
The Ride Down Mt. Morgan

ONE-ACT PLAYS

A View from the Bridge, *one-act version, with* A Memory of Two Mondays
Elegy for a Lady (*in* Two-Way Mirror)
Some Kind of Love Story (*in* Two-Way Mirror)
I Can't Remember Anything (*in* Danger: Memory!)
Clara (*in* Danger: Memory!)
The Last Yankee

OTHER WORKS

Situation Normal
The Misfits (*a cinema novel*)
Focus (*a novel*)
I Don't Need You Anymore (*short stories*)
Theatre Essays
Chinese Encounters (*reportage with Inge Morath photographs*)
In the Country (*reportage with Inge Morath photographs*)
In Russia (*reportage with Inge Morath photographs*)
Salesman in Beijing (*a memoir*)
Timebends (*autobiography*)

COLLECTIONS

Arthur Miller's Collected Plays (Volumes I and II)
The Portable Arthur Miller
The Theater Essays of Arthur Miller (*Robert Martin, editor*)

VIKING CRITICAL LIBRARY EDITIONS

Death of a Salesman (*edited by Gerald Weales*)
The Crucible (*edited by Gerald Weales*)

TELEVISION

Playing for Time

SCREENPLAYS

The Misfits
Everybody Wins
The Crucible

Broken Glass

Title p. 41
, 27

Nazi pre-occupation p. 11, 19, 24, 33, 34, 35, 49, 71, 84, 119, 121, 123, 127

ARTHUR MILLER

Is it my fault?
26 29
53
80 ff 139, 146, 151, 155

Sylvia's nightmare
110
128

Don't say
5 14 22

Willie Loman
134

She's trying to destroy me
89 92
139-140

Impotence
55 85 115-117
130 Blames Sylvia

Wanamaker's
60   101
132f

Sylvia walks
123, 127
157-158

Anti-semitism
138 150

PENGUIN BOOKS Becky Jewish - full-time job

PENGUIN BOOKS
Published by the Penguin Group
Penguin Books USA Inc., 375 Hudson Street,
New York, New York 10014, U.S.A.
Penguin Books Ltd, 27 Wrights Lane,
London W8 5TZ, England
Penguin Books Australia Ltd, Ringwood,
Victoria, Australia
Penguin Books Canada Ltd, 10 Alcorn Avenue,
Toronto, Ontario, Canada M4V 3B2
Penguin Books (N.Z.) Ltd, 182–190 Wairau Road,
Auckland 10, New Zealand

Penguin Books Ltd, Registered Offices:
Harmondsworth, Middlesex, England

First published in Penguin Books 1994

1 3 5 7 9 10 8 6 4 2

Library of Congress Cataloging in Publication Data
Miller, Arthur.
Broken glass : a play / by Arthur Miller.
p. cm.
ISBN 0 14 048.095 1
1. Holocaust, Jewish (1939–1945)—Foreign public opinion,
American—Drama.   2. Jewish men—New York (N.Y.)—Drama.
3. Marriage—New York (N.Y.)—Drama.   4. Bankers—New York (N.Y.)—
Drama.   I. Title.
PS3525.I5156B76   1994
812'.52—dc20   93-20949

Printed in the United States of America
Set in Bembo

To Inge Morath

The play takes place in Brooklyn in the last days of November 1938.

CAST OF CHARACTERS

Phillip Gellburg

Sylvia Gellburg

Dr. Harry Hyman

Margaret Hyman

Harriet

Stanton Case

Act One

SCENE ONE

A lone cellist is discovered, playing a simple tune.
The tune finishes. Light goes out on the cellist and
rises on. . . .

Office of Dr. Harry Hyman in his home. Alone on
stage Phillip Gellburg, a slender, intense man in his
late forties, waits in perfect stillness, legs crossed. He
is in a black suit, black tie and shoes and white shirt
and holds his black hat on his lap.

Margaret Hyman, the doctor's wife, enters. She is
fair, lusty, energetic, carries a pruning shears.

MARGARET: He'll be right with you, he's just changing. Can
I get you something? Tea?

GELLBURG, *faint reprimand:* He said seven o'clock sharp.

MARGARET: He was held up in the hospital, that new
union's pulled a strike, imagine? A strike in a hospital? It's
incredible. And his horse went lame.

GELLBURG: His horse?

MARGARET: He rides on Ocean Parkway every evening.

GELLBURG, *attempting easy familiarity:* Oh yes, I heard about that . . . it's very nice. You're Mrs. Hyman?

MARGARET: I've nodded to you on the street for years now, but you're too preoccupied to notice.

GELLBURG, *a barely hidden boast:* Lot on my mind, usually. *A certain amused loftiness.*—So you're his nurse, too.

MARGARET: We met in Mount Sinai when he was interning. He's lived to regret it. *She laughs in a burst.*

GELLBURG: That's some laugh you've got there. I sometimes hear you all the way down the block to my house.

MARGARET: Can't help it, my whole family does it. I'm originally from Minnesota. It's nice to meet you finally, Mr. Goldberg.

GELLBURG: —It's Gellburg, not Goldberg.

MARGARET: Oh, I'm sorry.

GELLBURG: G-e-l-l-b-u-r-g. It's the only one in the phone book.

MARGARET: It does sound like Goldberg.

GELLBURG: But it's not, it's Gellburg. *A distinction.* We're from Finland originally.

MARGARET: Oh! We came from Lithuania . . . Kazauskis?

GELLBURG, *put down momentarily:* Don't say.

MARGARET, *trying to charm him to his ease:* Ever been to Minnesota?

GELLBURG: New York State's the size of France, what would I go to Minnesota for?

MARGARET: Nothing. Just there's a lot of Finns there.

GELLBURG: Well there's Finns all over.

MARGARET, *defeated, shows the clipper.* . . . I'll get back to my roses. Whatever it is, I hope you'll be feeling better.

GELLBURG: It's not me.

MARGARET: Oh. 'Cause you seem a little pale.

GELLBURG: Me?—I'm always this color. It's my wife.

MARGARET: I'm sorry to hear that, she's a lovely woman. It's nothing serious, is it?

GELLBURG: He's just had a specialist put her through some tests, I'm waiting to hear. I think it's got him mystified.

MARGARET: Well, I mustn't butt in. *Makes to leave but can't resist.* Can you say what it is?

GELLBURG: She can't walk.

MARGARET: What do you mean?

GELLBURG, *an overtone of protest of some personal victimization:*
Can't stand up. No feeling in her legs.—I'm sure it'll pass,
but it's terrible.

MARGARET: But I only saw her in the grocery . . . can't be
more than ten days ago . . .

GELLBURG: It's nine days today.

MARGARET: But she's such a wonderful-looking woman.
Does she have fever?

GELLBURG: No.

MARGARET: Thank God, then it's not polio.

GELLBURG: No, she's in perfect health otherwise.

MARGARET: Well Harry'll get to the bottom of it if anybody
can. They call him from everywhere for opinions, you
know . . . Boston, Chicago . . . By rights he ought to be
on Park Avenue if he only had the ambition, but he always wanted a neighborhood practice. Why, I don't
know—we never invite anybody, we never go out, all
our friends are in Manhattan. But it's his nature, you can't
fight a person's nature. —You're not much of a talker,
are you.

GELLBURG, *purse-mouthed smile.* When I can get a word in edgewise.

MARGARET, *burst of laughter:* Ha!—so you've got a sense of humor after all. Well give my best to Mrs. Goldberg.

GELLBURG: Gellbu . . .

MARGARET, *hits her own head.* Gellburg, excuse me! —It practically sounds like Goldberg . . .

GELLBURG: No-no, look in the phone book, it's the only one, G-e-l-l . . .

Enter Dr. Hyman.

MARGARET, *with a little wave to Gellburg:* Be seeing you!

GELLBURG: Be in good health.

She exits.

HYMAN, *in his early fifties, a conventionally handsome man, but underneath a determined scientific idealist. Settling behind his desk—chuckling:* She chew your ear off?

GELLBURG, *his worldly mode:* Not too bad, I've had worse.

HYMAN: Well there's no way around it, women are talkers . . . *Grinning familiarly:* But try living without them, right?

GELLBURG: Without women?

HYMAN, *he sees Gellburg has flushed; there is a short hiatus, then:*
. . . Well, never mind. —I'm glad you could make it
tonight, I wanted to talk to you before I see your wife
again tomorrow. Smoke?

GELLBURG: No thanks, never have. Isn't it bad for you?

HYMAN: Certainly is. *Lights a cigar.* But more people die of
rat bite, you know.

GELLBURG: Rat bite!

HYMAN: Oh yes, but they're mostly the poor so it's not an
interesting statistic. Have you seen her tonight or d'you
come here from the office?

GELLBURG: I thought I'd see you before I went home.
But I phoned her this afternoon—same thing, no
change.

HYMAN: Did you get a bed put into the dining room?

GELLBURG: My son's; he's away in the army.

HYMAN: She told me. How's she doing with the wheelchair?

GELLBURG: Better, she can get herself in and out of the bed now.

HYMAN: Good. And she manages the bathroom?

GELLBURG: Oh yes. I got the maid to come in the mornings to help her take a bath, clean up . . .

HYMAN: Good. Your wife has a lot of courage, I admire that kind of woman. My wife is similar; I like the type.

GELLBURG: What type you mean?

HYMAN: You know—vigorous. I mean mentally and . . . you know, just generally. Moxie.

GELLBURG: Oh.

HYMAN: Forget it, it was only a remark.

GELLBURG: No, you're right, I never thought of it, but she is unusual that way.

HYMAN, *pause. Some prickliness here which he can't understand.* Doctor Sherman's report . . .

GELLBURG: What's he say?

HYMAN: I'm getting to it.

GELLBURG: Oh. Beg your pardon.

HYMAN: You'll have to bear with me . . . may I call you Phillip?

GELLBURG: Certainly.

HYMAN: I don't express my thoughts very quickly, Phillip.

GELLBURG: Likewise. Go ahead, take your time.

HYMAN: People tend to overestimate the wisdom of physicians so I try to think things through before I speak to a patient.

GELLBURG: I'm glad to hear that.

HYMAN: Aesculapius stuttered, you know—ancient Greek god of medicine. But probably based on a real physician who hesitated about giving advice. Somerset Maugham had a clubfoot, studied medicine. Or some character of his did, I forget . . . oh yes, *Human Bondage*—but I don't imagine you've read that. Anton Chekhov, great writer, had tuberculosis. Doctors are very often physically defective in some way, that's why they're interested in healing. *A certain portentousness.* —This is all psychology.

GELLBURG, *impressed:* I see.

HYMAN: I'll tell you why I'm saying all this; it's that we are in the realm of psychology with your wife, Phillip. And we have to proceed with great caution when we approach the mind.

GELLBURG: I'm glad to hear you say that. —I've been thinking the same thing—I think this was brought on by some
kind of scare.

HYMAN: Well that's interesting, let's talk about that in a
minute. *Pause. Thinks.* I find this Adolf Hitler very disturbing. You been following him in the papers?

GELLBURG: Well yes, but not much. My average day in the
office is ten, eleven hours.

HYMAN: They've been smashing the Jewish stores in Berlin
all week, you know.

GELLBURG: Oh yes, I saw that again yesterday.

HYMAN: Very disturbing. Forcing old men to scrub the sidewalks with toothbrushes. On the Kurfürstendamm, that's
equivalent to Fifth Avenue. Nothing but hoodlums in uni-
form.

GELLBURG: My wife is very upset about that.

HYMAN: I know, that's why I mention it. *Hesitates* . . . And
how about you?

GELLBURG: Of course. It's a terrible thing. Why do you ask?

HYMAN, *a smile:* —I don't know, I got the feeling she may
be afraid she's annoying you when she talks about such
things.

GELLBURG: Why? I don't mind. —She said she's annoy-ing me?

HYMAN: Not in so many words, but . . .

GELLBURG: I can't believe she'd say a thing like . . .

HYMAN: Wait a minute, I didn't say she said it . . .

GELLBURG: She doesn't annoy me, but what can be done about such things? The thing is, she doesn't like to hear about the other side of it.

HYMAN: What other side?

GELLBURG: It's no excuse for what's happening over there, but German Jews can be pretty . . . you know . . . *Pushes up his nose with his forefinger.* Not that they're pushy like the ones from Poland or Russia but friend of mine's in the garment industry; these German Jews won't take an ordinary good job, you know; it's got to be pretty high up in the firm or they're insulted. And they can't even speak English.

HYMAN: Well I guess a lot of them were pretty important over there.

GELLBURG: I know, but they're supposed to be *refugees,* aren't they? With all our unemployment you'd think they'd appreciate a little more. Latest official figure is twelve million unemployed you know, and it's probably bigger but Roosevelt can't admit it, after the fortune he's pouring into WPA and the rest of that welfare *mishugas.* —But she's not *annoying* me, for God's sake.

HYMAN: . . . I just thought I'd mention it; but it was only a feeling I had . . .

GELLBURG: I'll tell you right now, I don't run with the crowd, I see with these eyes, nobody else's.

HYMAN: I see that. —You're very unusual— *Grinning.* — you almost sound like a Republican.

GELLBURG: Why?—the Torah says a Jew has to be a Democrat? I didn't get where I am by agreeing with everybody.

HYMAN: Well that's a good thing; you're independent. *Nods, puffs.* You know, what mystifies me is that the Germans I knew in Heidelberg . . . I took my M.D. there . . .

GELLBURG: You got along with them.

HYMAN: Some of the finest people I ever met.

GELLBURG: Well there you go.

HYMAN: We had a marvelous student choral group, fantastic voices; Saturday nights, we'd have a few beers and go singing through the streets. . . . People'd applaud from the windows.

GELLBURG: Don't say.

HYMAN: I simply can't imagine those people marching into Austria, and now they say Czechoslovakia's next, and Poland. . . . But fanatics have taken Germany, I guess, and they can be brutal, you know . . .

GELLBURG: Listen, I sympathize with these refugees, but . . .

HYMAN, *cutting him off*: I had quite a long talk with Sylvia yesterday, I suppose she told you?

GELLBURG, *a tensing* . . . Well . . . no, she didn't mention. What about?

HYMAN, *surprised by Sylvia's omission*: . . . Well about her condition, and . . . just in passing . . . your relationship.

GELLBURG, *flushing: My* relationship?

HYMAN: . . . It was just in passing.

GELLBURG: Why, what'd she say?

HYMAN: Well that you . . . get along very well.

GELLBURG: Oh.

HYMAN, *encouragingly, as he sees Gellburg's small tension*: I found her a remarkably well informed woman. Especially for this neighborhood.

GELLBURG, *a pridefully approving nod; relieved that he can speak of her positively:* That's practically why we got together in the first place. I don't exaggerate, if Sylvia was a man she could have run the Federal Reserve. You could talk to Sylvia like you talk to a man.

HYMAN: I'll bet.

GELLBURG, *his purse-mouthed grin:* . . . Not that talking was all we did—but you turn your back on Sylvia and she's got her nose in a book or a magazine. I mean there's not one woman in ten around here could even tell you who their congressman is. And you can throw in the men, too. *Pause.* So where are we?

HYMAN: Doctor Sherman confirms my diagnosis. I ask you to listen carefully, will you?

GELLBURG, *brought up:* Of course, that's why I came.

HYMAN: We can find no physical reason for her inability to walk.

GELLBURG: No physical reason . . .

HYMAN: We are almost certain that this is a psychological condition.

GELLBURG: But she's numb, she has no feeling in her legs.

HYMAN: Yes. This is what we call an hysterical paralysis. Hysterical doesn't mean she screams and yells . . .

GELLBURG: Oh, I know. It means like . . . ah . . . *Bumbles off.*

HYMAN, *a flash of umbrage, dislike.* Let me explain what it means, okay?—Hysteria comes from the Greek word for the womb because it was thought to be a symptom of female anxiety. Of course it isn't, but that's where it comes from. People who are anxious enough or really frightened can imagine they've gone blind or deaf, for instance . . . and they really can't see or hear. It was sometimes called shell shock during the War.

GELLBURG: You mean . . . you don't mean she's . . . crazy.

HYMAN: We'll have to talk turkey, Phillip. If I'm going to do you any good I have to know more about Sylvia . . . and you, too, naturally. I'm going to have to ask you some personal questions. Some of them may sound raw, but I've only been superficially acquainted with Sylvia's family and I need to know more . . .

GELLBURG: She says you treated her father . . .

HYMAN: Briefly; a few visits shortly before he passed away. They're fine people. I hate like hell to see this happen to her, you see what I mean?

GELLBURG: You can tell it to me; is she crazy?

HYMAN: Phillip, are you? Am I? In one way or another, who isn't crazy? The main difference is that our kind of crazy still allows us to walk around and tend to our business. But who knows?—people like us may be the craziest of all.

GELLBURG, *scoffing grin:* Why!

HYMAN: Because we don't know we're nuts, and the other kind does.

GELLBURG: I don't know about that . . .

HYMAN: Well, it's neither here nor there.

GELLBURG: I certainly don't think *I'm* nuts.

HYMAN: I wasn't saying that . . .

GELLBURG: What do you mean, then?

HYMAN, *grinning:* You're not an easy man to talk to, are you.

GELLBURG: Why? If I don't understand I have to ask, don't I?

HYMAN: Yes, you're right.

GELLBURG: That's the way I am—they don't pay me for being easy to talk to.

HYMAN: You're in . . . real estate?

GELLBURG: I'm head of the Mortgage Department of Brooklyn Guarantee and Trust.

HYMAN: Oh, that's right, she told me.

GELLBURG: We are the largest lender east of the Mississippi.

HYMAN: Really. *Fighting deflation.* Well let me tell you my approach; if possible I'd like to keep her out of that whole psychiatry rigmarole. Not that I'm against it, but I think you get further faster, sometimes, with a little common sense and some plain human sympathy. Can we talk turkey? *Tuchas offen tisch,* you know any Yiddish?

GELLBURG: Get your ass on the table.

HYMAN: Correct. So let's forget crazy and try to face the facts. We have a strong, healthy woman who has no physical ailment, and suddenly can't stand on her legs. Why?

He goes silent. Gellburg shifts uneasily.

I don't mean to embarrass you . . .

GELLBURG, *an angry smile.* You're not embarrassing me. — What do you want to know?

HYMAN, *sets himself, then launches:* In these cases there is often a sexual disability. You have relations, I imagine?

GELLBURG: Relations? Yes, we have relations.

HYMAN, *a softening smile.* Often?

GELLBURG: What's that got to do with it?

HYMAN: Sex could be connected. You don't have to answer . . .

GELLBURG: No-no it's all right. . . . I would say it depends—maybe twice, three times a week.

HYMAN, *seems surprised.* Well that's good. She seems satisfied?

GELLBURG, *shrugs; hostilely:* I guess she is, sure.

HYMAN: That was a foolish question, forget it.

GELLBURG, *flushed:* Why, did she mention something about this?

HYMAN: Oh no, it's just something I thought of later.

GELLBURG: Well, I'm no Rudolph Valentino but I . . .

HYMAN: Rudolph Valentino probably isn't either. —You mentioned she got scared. What of, you have any idea?

GELLBURG, *relieved to be off the other subject:* If you ask me I think it was when they started putting all the pictures in the paper. About these Nazi carryings-on. I noticed she started . . . staring at them . . . in a very peculiar way. And . . . I don't know, I think she got harder to talk to.

HYMAN: . . . Harder for you.

GELLBURG: Yes. It made her angry or something.

HYMAN: At you.

GELLBURG: Well . . . *Nods, agreeing* . . . in general. — Personally I don't think they should be publishing those kind of pictures.

HYMAN: Why not?

GELLBURG: She scares herself to death with them—six thousand miles away, and what does it accomplish! Except maybe put some fancy new ideas into these anti-Semites walking around New York here.

Slight pause.

HYMAN: Tell me how she collapsed. You were going to the movies . . . ?

GELLBURG, *breathing more deeply:* Yes. We were just starting down the porch steps and all of a sudden her . . . *Difficulty; he breaks off.*

HYMAN: I'm sorry but I . . .

GELLBURG: . . . Her legs turned to butter. I couldn't stand her up. Kept falling around like a rag doll. I had to carry her into the house. And she kept apologizing . . . ! *He weeps; recovers.* I can't talk about it.

HYMAN: It's all right.

GELLBURG: She's always been such a level-headed woman. *Weeping threatens again.* I don't know what to do. She's my life.

HYMAN: I'll do my best for her, Phillip, she's a wonderful woman. —Let's talk about something else. What do you do exactly?

GELLBURG: I mainly evaluate properties.

HYMAN: Whether to grant a mortgage . . .

GELLBURG: And how big a one and the terms.

HYMAN: How's the Depression hit you?

GELLBURG: Well, it's no comparison with '32 to '36, let's say—we were foreclosing left and right in those days. It's not like the twenties, of course, but we're on our feet and running.

HYMAN: And you head the department . . .

GELLBURG: Above me is only Mr. Case.

HYMAN: Mr. Case is . . . ?

GELLBURG: Stanton Wylie Case; he's chairman and president. You're not interested in boat racing.

HYMAN: Why?

GELLBURG: His yacht won the America's Cup two years ago. For the second time. The *Aurora*?

HYMAN: Oh yes! I think I read about . . .

GELLBURG: He's had me aboard twice.

HYMAN: Really.

GELLBURG, *the grin*. The only Jew ever set foot on that deck.

HYMAN: Don't say.

GELLBURG: In fact, I'm the only Jew ever worked for Brooklyn Guarantee in their whole history.

HYMAN: That so.

GELLBURG: Oh yes. And they go back to the 1890s. Started right out of accountancy school and moved straight up. They've been wonderful to me; it's a great firm.

HYMAN: Sylvia go along on the boat?

GELLBURG: Oh God no, just Mr. Case and a few friends and the crew. Women are bad luck on racing boats, you know. —Although at the beginning of the season he sometimes takes Mrs. Case . . . just, you know, for the afternoon.

> *A long moment as Hyman stares at Gellburg, who is proudly positioned now, absorbing his poise from the evoked memories of his success. Gradually Gellburg turns to him.*

How could this be a mental condition?

HYMAN: It's unconscious; like . . . well take yourself; I notice you only wear black. Can I ask you why?

GELLBURG: I've worn black since high school.

HYMAN: No particular reason.

GELLBURG, *shrugs.* Always liked it, that's all.

HYMAN: Well it's a similar thing with her; she doesn't know why she's doing this, but some very deep, hidden part of her mind is directing her to do it. You don't agree.

GELLBURG: I don't know.

HYMAN: You think she knows what she's doing?

GELLBURG: Well I always liked black for business reasons.

HYMAN: It gives you authority?

GELLBURG: Not exactly authority, but . . . See, I graduated high school at fifteen and I was only twenty-two when I entered the firm. So I wanted to look a little older. But I knew what I was doing.

HYMAN: Then you think she's doing this on purpose?

GELLBURG:—Except she's numb; nobody can purposely do that, can they?

HYMAN: I don't think so. But why would she want to do this to herself?

GELLBURG, *he stares into space, then shakes his head.* . . . Well maybe . . . *Breaks off.* I can't imagine.

HYMAN: We may as well talk about it—if you have an idea. What were you going to say?

GELLBURG: Well . . . so the Nazis couldn't get to her. — But that's ridiculous.

HYMAN: How would getting paralyzed protect her from the Nazis?

GELLBURG: That's what I say, it's ridiculous.

HYMAN: Let's talk about it anyway—lots of things are ridiculous but they happen. —How would a paralysis protect her?

GELLBURG: . . . It was just an idea, I don't know why. I mean they're three thousand miles away.

HYMAN: Yes. *Pause.* —I tell you, Phillip, not really knowing your wife, if there's anything you could tell me about . . . you know . . . what reason she could have for doing a thing like this . . .

GELLBURG: I told you, I don't know.

HYMAN: Nothing occurs to you.

GELLBURG, *an edge of irritation:* I can't think of anything.

HYMAN: I tell you a funny thing that struck me about her.

GELLBURG: What.

HYMAN: Talking to her, she doesn't seem all that unhappy.

GELLBURG: Say!—yes, that's what I mean. That's exactly what I mean. It's like she's almost . . . I don't know . . . enjoying herself. I mean in a way.

HYMAN: How could that be possible?

GELLBURG: Of course she apologizes for it, and for making it hard for me—you know, like I have to do a lot of the cooking now, and tending to my laundry and so on . . . I even shop for groceries and the butcher . . . and change the sheets . . .

He breaks off with some realization. Hyman doesn't speak. A long pause.

You mean . . . she's doing it against me?

HYMAN: I don't know, what do *you* think?

GELLBURG, *stares for a long moment, then makes to rise, obviously deeply disturbed.* I'd better be getting home.

HYMAN: . . . There's just a couple of points, if you have time.

GELLBURG: I'm very tired . . .

HYMAN:—You have the one son?

GELLBURG: In the army, yes. Artillery man. Jerome. He's a captain.

HYMAN: That's surprising, a Jewish boy going into the army in peacetime.

GELLBURG: I'd loved to have gone in myself when I was his age but I had to earn money. My parents were turning fifty when I was born so I had to support them.

HYMAN: Then the army was your idea.

GELLBURG: You could say that. He's got a good chance to end up on General MacArthur's staff. The general speaks to him now and then. Not officially, of course, but . . . you know, shows his friendliness. He's the only Jewish captain in the army.

HYMAN: Huh!

GELLBURG: MacArthur's crazy about him.

HYMAN, *a long pause.* I wonder what could be frightening your wife.

GELLBURG: I can't imagine.

HYMAN: Well let's talk again after I see her tomorrow. Maybe I should tell you . . . I have this unconventional approach to illness, Phillip. Especially where the mental element is involved. I believe we get sick in twos and threes, not alone as individuals. I even wonder if people get cancer alone. You follow me?

GELLBURG, *lost in his own thought:* I don't know whether to ask you this or not.

HYMAN: What's to lose, go ahead.

GELLBURG: My parents were from the old country, and my
    mother used to tell me—I don't know if it was a story or
    something that happened—but I think it was in Poland
    someplace or—not that I believe in such things—but
    there was this woman who they say was . . . you know . . .
    gotten into by a . . . like the ghost of a dead person . . .

HYMAN: A dybbuk.

GELLBURG: That's it. And it made her lose her mind and so
    forth. —You believe in that? They had to get a rabbi to
    pray it out of her body. But you think that's possible?

HYMAN: Do I think so? No. Do you?

GELLBURG: Oh no. It just crossed my mind.

HYMAN: Well I wouldn't know how to pray it out of
    her, so . . .

GELLBURG: Be straight with me—is she going to come out
    of this?

HYMAN: I want you to do me a favor, will you?

GELLBURG: What's that.

HYMAN: You won't be offended, okay?

GELLBURG, *tensely:* Why should I be offended?

HYMAN: I'd like you to give her a lot of loving. *Fixing Gell-burg in his gaze.* Can you? It's important now.

GELLBURG: Say, you're not blaming this on me, are you?

HYMAN: What's the good of blame? —from here on out, *tuchas offen tisch,* okay?—everything on the table. And Phillip?

GELLBURG: Yes?

HYMAN, *a light chuckle:* Try not to let yourself get mad.

> *Gellburg turns and goes out. Hyman returns to his desk, makes some notes. Margaret enters.*

MARGARET: That's one miserable little pisser.

> *He writes, doesn't look up.*

He's a dictator, you know. I was just remembering when I went to the grandmother's funeral? He stands outside the funeral parlor and decides who's going to sit with who in the limousines for the cemetery. "You sit with him, you sit with her . . ." And they obey him like he owned the funeral!

HYMAN: Did you find out what's playing?

MARGARET: At the Beverly they've got Ginger Rogers and Fred Astaire. Jimmy Cagney's at the Rialto but it's another gangster story.

HYMAN: I have a sour feeling about this damned thing. I barely know my way around psychology, I don't know why I got into it.

MARGARET: You know why you got into it.

HYMAN: It's always the same thing with you.

MARGARET: No, with you.

HYMAN: I'm not interested in Mrs. Gellburg.

MARGARET: Since when?

HYMAN: I hardly know her!

MARGARET: Since when do you have to know them? You're a hopeless case, Harry. If we're going we'll have to leave now. I'd rather see the Fred Astaire.

HYMAN: Come here. *He reaches out, draws her to him by the hand.* You're the best, Margaret.

MARGARET: A lot of good it does me.

He stands, gets behind her, and is gradually bending her forward over the desk as he kisses her neck.

MARGARET: Please don't get involved, Harry.

HYMAN: If you want, I'll get someone else to take the case.

MARGARET: You won't, you know you won't . . .

He is lifting her skirt.

Don't, Harry. Come on . . .

She frees her skirt. He kisses her breasts . . .

HYMAN: God Almighty, Margaret, how I love you.

Blackout.

SCENE TWO

The Lone Cellist plays. Then lights go down . . .

Next evening. The Gellburg house. Sylvia Gellburg is seated in a wheelchair reading a newspaper. Beside her, an upholstered chair. She is in her mid-forties, a buxom, capable, and warm woman. Right now her hair is brushed down to her shoulders, and she is in a nightgown and robe.

She reads the paper with an intense, almost haunted interest, looking up now and then to visualize.

Her sister Harriet, a couple of years younger, enters. Wears a spring dress and carries a pocketbook.

HARRIET: So what do you want, steak or chicken? Or maybe he'd like chops for a change.

SYLVIA: Please, don't put yourself out, Phillip doesn't mind a little shopping.

HARRIET: What's the matter with you, I'm going anyway, he's got enough on his mind.

SYLVIA: Well all right, get a couple of chops.

HARRIET: And what about you. You have to start eating!

SYLVIA: I'm eating.

HARRIET: What, a piece of cucumber? Look how pale you
   are. And what is this with newspapers night and day?

SYLVIA: I like to see what's happening.

HARRIET: I don't know about this doctor. Maybe you need
   a specialist.

SYLVIA: He brought one two days ago, Doctor Sherman.
   From Mount Sinai.

HARRIET: Really? And?

SYLVIA: We're waiting to hear. I like Doctor Hyman.

HARRIET: Nobody in the family ever had anything like this.
   You feel *something*, though, don't you?

SYLVIA, *pause. She lifts her face.* Yes . . . but inside, not on
   the skin. *Looks at her legs.* I can harden the muscles but I
   can't lift them. *Strokes her thighs.* I seem to have an ache.
   Not only here but . . . *She runs her hands down her trunk.*
   My whole body seems . . . I can't describe it. It's like I
   was just born and . . . didn't want to come out yet. Like
   a deep, terrible aching . . .

HARRIET: Didn't want to come out yet! What are you talking about?

SYLVIA, *sighs gently, knowing Harriet can never understand.* Maybe if he has a nice duck. If not, get the chops. And thanks, Harriet, it's sweet of you. *She returns to her newspaper.*

HARRIET: I wish I knew what is suddenly so interesting in a newspaper. This is not normal, Sylvia, is it?

SYLVIA, *pause. She stares ahead.* They are making old men crawl around and clean the sidewalks with toothbrushes.

HARRIET: Who is?

SYLVIA: In Germany. Old men with beards!

HARRIET: So why are you so interested in that?

SYLVIA, *slight pause; searches within.* I don't really know. *A slight pause.* Remember Grandpa? His eyeglasses with the bent sidepiece? One of the old men in the paper was his spitting image, he had the same exact glasses with the wire frames. I can't get it out of my mind. On their knees on the sidewalk, two old men. And there's fifteen or twenty people standing in a circle laughing at them scrubbing with toothbrushes. There's three women in the picture; they're holding their coat collars closed, so it must have been cold . . .

HARRIET: Why would they make them scrub with tooth-brushes?

SYLVIA, *angered:* To humiliate them, to make fools of them!

HARRIET: Oh!

SYLVIA: How can you be so . . . so . . . ? *Breaks off before she goes too far.* Harriet, please . . . leave me alone, will you?

HARRIET: This is not normal. Murray says the same thing. I swear to God, he came home last night and says, "She's got to stop thinking about those Germans." And you know how he loves current events. *Sylvia is staring ahead.* I'll see if the duck looks good, if not I'll get chops. Can I get you something now?

SYLVIA: No, I'm fine, thanks.

HARRIET: I'm going. *Moves upstage of Sylvia.*

SYLVIA: Yes.

> *She returns to her paper. Harriet watches anxiously for a moment, out of Sylvia's sight line, then exits. Sylvia turns a page, absorbed in the paper. Suddenly she turns in shock—Phillip is standing behind her. He holds a small paper bag.*

SYLVIA: Oh! I didn't hear you come in.

GELLBURG: I tiptoed, in case you were dozing off . . . *His dour smile.* I bought you some sour pickles.

SYLVIA: Oh, that's nice. Later, maybe. You have one.

GELLBURG: I'll wait. *Awkwardly but determined:* I was passing Greenberg's on Flatbush Avenue and I suddenly remembered how you used to love them. Remember?

SYLVIA: Thanks, that's nice of you. What were you doing on Flatbush Avenue?

GELLBURG: There's a property across from A&S. I'm probably going to foreclose.

SYLVIA: Oh that's sad. Are they nice people?

GELLBURG, *shrugs.* People are people—I gave them two extensions but they'll never manage . . . nothing up here. *Taps his temple.*

SYLVIA: Aren't you early?

GELLBURG: I got worried about you. Doctor come?

SYLVIA: He called; he has the results of the tests but he wants to come tomorrow when he has more time to talk to me. He's really very nice.

GELLBURG: How was it today?

SYLVIA: I'm so sorry about this.

GELLBURG: You'll get better, don't worry about it. Oh!—
there's a letter from the captain. *Takes it out of his jacket.*

SYLVIA: Jerome?

GELLBURG, *terrific personal pride:* Read it.

> *She reads; his purse-mouthed grin is intense.*

That's your son.

SYLVIA: Fort Sill?

GELLBURG: Oklahoma. *He's going to lecture them on artillery!*
In *Fort Sill!* That's the field-artillery center.

> *She looks up dumbly.*

That's like being invited to the Vatican to lecture the
Pope.

SYLVIA: Imagine. *She folds the letter and hands it back to him.*

PHILLIP, *restraining greater resentment:* I don't understand this
attitude.

SYLVIA: Why? I'm happy for him.

PHILLIP: You don't seem happy to me.

SYLVIA: I'll never get used to it. Who goes in the army? Men who can't do anything else.

PHILLIP: I wanted people to see that a Jew doesn't have to be a lawyer or a doctor or a businessman.

SYLVIA: That's fine, but why must it be Jerome?

PHILLIP: You don't seem to realize—he could be the first Jewish general in the United States Army. Doesn't it mean something to be his mother?

SYLVIA, *with an edge of resentment:* Well, I said I'm glad.

GELLBURG: Don't be upset. *Looks about impatiently.* You know, when you get on your feet I'll help you hang the new drapes.

SYLVIA: I started to . . .

PHILLIP: But they've been here over a month.

SYLVIA: Well this happened, I'm sorry.

PHILLIP: You have to occupy yourself is all I'm saying, Sylvia, you can't give in to this.

SYLVIA, *near an outburst:* Well I'm sorry—I'm sorry about everything!

PHILLIP: Please, don't get upset, I take it back!

A moment; stalemate.

SYLVIA: I wonder what my tests show.

He is silent.

That the specialist did.

PHILLIP: I went to see him last night.

SYLVIA: You did? Why didn't you mention it?

PHILLIP: I wanted to think over what he said.

SYLVIA: What did he say?

> *With a certain deliberateness, Phillip goes over to her
> and gives her a kiss on the cheek.*

SYLVIA, *she is embarrassed and vaguely alarmed.* Phillip! *A little
uncomprehending laugh.*

PHILLIP: I want to change some things. About the way I've
been doing.

> *He stands there for a moment perfectly still, then rolls
> her chair closer to the upholstered chair in which he
> now sits and takes her hand. She doesn't quite know
> what to make of this, but doesn't remove her hand.*

SYLVIA: Well what did he say?

GELLBURG, *he pats her hand.* I'll tell you in a minute. I'm thinking about a Dodge.

SYLVIA: A Dodge?

GELLBURG: I want to teach you to drive. So you can go where you like, visit your mother in the afternoon. —I want you to be happy, Sylvia.

SYLVIA, *surprised:* Oh.

GELLBURG: We have the money, we could do a lot of things. Maybe see Washington, D.C. It's supposed to be a very strong car, you know.

SYLVIA: But aren't they all black?—Dodges?

GELLBURG: Not all. I've seen a couple of green ones.

SYLVIA: You like green?

GELLBURG: It's only a color. You'll get used to it. —Or Chicago.

SYLVIA: Tell me what Hyman said.

GELLBURG, *gets himself set.* He thinks it could all be coming from your mind. Like . . . a fear of some kind got into you. Psychological.

She is still, listening.

Are you afraid of something?

SYLVIA, *a slow shrug, a shake of her head.* . . . I don't know,
I don't think so. What kind of fear, what does he mean?

GELLBURG: Well, he explains it better, but . . . like in a war,
people get so afraid they go blind temporarily. What they
call shell shock. But once they feel safer it goes away.

SYLVIA, *thinks about this a moment.* What about the tests the
Mount Sinai man did?

GELLBURG: They can't find anything wrong with your body.

SYLVIA: But I'm numb!

GELLBURG: He claims being very frightened could be doing
it. —Are you?

SYLVIA: I don't know.

GELLBURG: Personally. . . . Can I tell you what I think?

SYLVIA: What.

GELLBURG: I think it's this whole Nazi business.

SYLVIA: But it's in the paper—they're smashing up the Jewish stores . . . Should I not read the paper? The streets are
covered with broken glass!

GELLBURG: Yes, but you don't have to be constantly . . .

SYLVIA: It's ridiculous. I can't move my legs from reading a newspaper?

GELLBURG: He didn't say that; but I'm wondering if you're too involved with . . .

SYLVIA: It's ridiculous.

GELLBURG: Well you talk to him tomorrow. *Pause. He comes back to her and takes her hand, his need open.* You've got to get better, Sylvia.

SYLVIA, *she sees his tortured face and tries to laugh.* What is this, am I dying or something?

GELLBURG: How can you say that?

SYLVIA: I've never seen such a look in your face.

GELLBURG: Oh no-no-no . . . I'm just worried.

SYLVIA: I don't understand what's happening . . . *She turns away on the verge of tears.*

GELLBURG: . . . I never realized . . . *Sudden sharpness:* . . . look at me, will you?

She turns to him; he glances down at the floor.

Too late for sex

I wouldn't know what to do without you, Sylvia, honest
to God. I . . . *Immense difficulty.* I love you.

SYLVIA, *a dead, bewildered laugh.* What is this?

GELLBURG: You have to get better. If I'm ever doing something wrong I'll change it. Let's try to be different. All
right? And you too, you've got to do what the doctors
tell you.

SYLVIA: What can I do? Here I sit and they say there's nothing wrong with me.

GELLBURG: Listen . . . I think Hyman is a very smart man
. . . *He lifts her hand and kisses her knuckle; embarrassed and
smiling* . . . When we were talking, something came to
mind; that maybe if we could sit down with him, the
three of us, and maybe talk about . . . you know . . .
everything.

Pause.

SYLVIA: That doesn't matter anymore, Phillip.

GELLBURG, *an embarrassed grin.* How do you know? Maybe . . .

SYLVIA: It's too late for that.

GELLBURG, *once launched he is terrified.* Why? Why is it too
late?

SYLVIA: I'm surprised you're still worried about it.

GELLBURG: I'm not worried, I just think about it now and then.

SYLVIA: Well it's too late, dear, it doesn't matter anymore. *She draws back her hand.*

Pause.

GELLBURG: I'd be willing to discuss it now, if you would.

SYLVIA: What's there to discuss? That's over, it doesn't matter anymore, it hasn't for years.

GELLBURG: . . . Well all right. But if you wanted to I'd . . .

SYLVIA: We did talk about it, we talked to Rabbi Steiner twice about it, what good did it do?

GELLBURG: In those days I still thought it would change by itself. I was so young, I didn't understand such things. It came out of nowhere and I thought it would go the same way.

SYLVIA: I'm sorry, Phillip, it didn't come out of nowhere.

Silent, he evades her eyes.

SYLVIA: You regretted you got married.

GELLBURG: I didn't "regret" it . . .

SYLVIA: You did, dear. You don't have to be ashamed of it.

A long silence.

GELLBURG: I'm going to tell you the truth—in those days I thought that if we separated I wouldn't die of it. I admit that.

SYLVIA: I always knew that.

GELLBURG: But I haven't felt that way in years now.

SYLVIA: Well I'm here. *Spreads her arms out, a wildly ironical look in her eyes.* Here I am, Phillip!

GELLBURG, *offended:* The way you say that is not very . . .

SYLVIA: Not very what? I'm here; I've been here a long time.

GELLBURG, *a helpless surge of anger:* I'm trying to tell you something!

SYLVIA, *openly taunting him now:* But I said I'm here!

He moves about as she speaks, as though trying to find an escape or a way in.

I'm here for my mother's sake, and Jerome's sake, and everybody's sake except mine, but I'm here and here I

am. And now finally you want to talk about it, now when
I'm turning into an old woman? How do you want me
to say it? Tell me, dear, I'll say it the way you want me
to. What should I say?

GELLBURG, *insulted and guilty:* I want you to stand up.

SYLVIA: I can't stand up.

> *He takes both her hands.*

GELLBURG: You can. Now come on. Stand up.

SYLVIA: I can't!

GELLBURG: You can stand up, Sylvia. Now lean to me and
get on your feet.

> *He pulls her up; then steps aside, releasing her; she
> collapses on the floor. He stands over her.*

What are you trying to do? *He goes to his knees to yell into
her face: What are you trying to do, Sylvia!*

> *She looks at him in terror at the mystery before her.*

> *Blackout.*

SCENE THREE

The Lone Cellist plays. Then lights go down . . .

Dr. Hyman's office. He is in riding clothes. Harriet is seated beside his desk.

HARRIET: My poor sister. And they have everything! But how can it be in the mind if she's so paralyzed?

HYMAN: Her numbness is random, it doesn't follow the nerve paths; only part of the thighs are affected, part of the calves, it makes no physiological sense.

HARRIET, *frightened, spooked:* How can this be?—she's always had the best brains of any of us . . .

HYMAN: It has nothing to do with that. Listen to me now; I'm trying to know her a little better, and I have a few things I'd like to ask you, all right?

HARRIET: You know, I'm glad it's you taking care of her, my husband says the same thing.

HYMAN: Thank you . . .

HARRIET: You probably don't remember, but you once took out our cousin Roslyn Fein? She said you were great.

HYMAN: Roslyn Fein. When?

HARRIET: She's very tall and reddish-blond hair? She had a real crush . . .

HYMAN, *pleased:* When was this?

HARRIET: Oh—NYU, maybe twenty-five years ago. She adored you; seriously, she said you were really *great*. *Laughs knowingly.* Used to take her to Coney Island swimming, and so on.

HYMAN, *laughs with her.* Oh. Well give her my regards.

HARRIET: I hardly see her, she lives in Florida.

HYMAN, *pressing on:* I'd like you to tell me about Sylvia; — before she collapsed, was there any sign of some shock, or a . . .

HARRIET: You know they were on their way to a movie . . .

HYMAN: I'm talking about before that—did she ever seem frightened or anything? Something threatening her?

HARRIET, *thinks for a moment, shrugs, shaking her head:* Listen, I'll tell you something funny—I don't know if I should

say this, but to me sometimes she seems . . . I was going to say happy, but it's more like . . . I don't know
. . . like satisfied. I mean since the collapse. Don't you
think so?

HYMAN: Well I never really knew her before, but I see what
you mean.

HARRIET: . . . For a second now and then, it even goes
through my mind that maybe this is how she wants to be.

HYMAN: Uh huh.

HARRIET: But how is that possible?

HYMAN: I don't know. —What about this fascination with
the Nazis—she ever talk to you about that?

HARRIET: Only this last couple of weeks. Suddenly she's
. . . I don't understand it, they're in *Germany*, how can
she be so frightened, it's across the ocean, isn't it?

HYMAN: Yes. But in a way it isn't. *He stares, shaking his head,
lost.*

HARRIET: What do you mean?

HYMAN: . . . She's very sensitive; she really sees the people
in those photographs. They're alive to her.

HARRIET, *suddenly near tears:* My poor sister!

HYMAN: Tell me about Phillip.

HARRIET: . . . Listen . . . I wish you'd tell me . . . is she crazy?

HYMAN: She's going to be all right. Tell me about him.

HARRIET: Phillip? *Shrugs*. Phillip is Phillip.

HYMAN: You like him?

HARRIET: Well he's my brother-in-law . . . You mean personally.

HYMAN: Yes.

HARRIET, *takes a breath to lie*. . . . He can be very sweet, you know. But suddenly he'll turn around and talk to you like you've got long ears and four legs. The men—not that they don't respect him—but they'd just as soon not play cards with him if they can help it.

HYMAN: Really. Why?

HARRIET: Well God forbid you have an opinion—you open your mouth and he gives you that Republican look down his nose and your brains dry up. Not that I don't *like* him . . .

HYMAN: How did he and Sylvia meet?

HARRIET: She was head bookkeeper at Empire Steel over there in Long Island City . . .

HYMAN: She must have been very young.

HARRIET: . . . Twenty; just out of high school, practically, and in hardly a year she's head bookkeeper. According to my husband, God gave Sylvia all the brains and the rest of us the big feet! The reason they met was the company took out a mortgage and she had to explain all the accounts to Phillip—he used to say, "I fell in love with her figures!"

HYMAN: So he has a sense of humor.

HARRIET: . . . Why should I lie?—personally to me, he's a little bit a prune. Like he never stops with the whole Jewish part of it.

HYMAN: He doesn't like being Jewish.

HARRIET: Well it depends—like Jerome being the only Jewish captain, he's proud of that. And him being the only one ever worked for Brooklyn Guarantee—he's proud of that too, but at the same time . . .

HYMAN: . . . He'd rather not be one.

HARRIET: . . . Look, he's a mystery to me. I don't understand him and I never will.

HYMAN: What about the marriage? I promise you this is strictly between us.

HARRIET: What can I tell you, the marriage is a marriage.

HYMAN: And?

HARRIET: I shouldn't talk about it.

HYMAN: It stays in this office. Tell me. They ever break up?

HARRIET: Oh God no! Why should they?

HYMAN: Well it sounds like a very troubled marriage.

HARRIET: Well yes, but he's a wonderful provider. There's no Depression for Phillip, you know. And it would kill our mother, she worships Phillip, she'd never outlive it. No-no, it's out of the question, Sylvia's not that kind of woman, although . . . *Breaks off.*

HYMAN: What.

HARRIET: . . . Well I guess everybody knows it, so . . . *Takes a breath.* I think they came very close to it one time . . . when he hit her with the steak.

HYMAN: Hit her with a *steak*?

SYLVIA: It was overdone.

HYMAN: What do you mean, hit her?

SYLVIA: He picked it up off the plate and slapped her in the face with it.

HYMAN: And then what?

HARRIET: Well if my mother hadn't patched it up I don't know what would have happened.

HYMAN: And what then?—they make up?

HARRIET: Well he went out and bought her that gorgeous beaver coat, and repainted the whole house, and he's tight as a drum, you know, so it was hard for him. I don't know what to tell you. —Why?—you think *he* could have frightened her like this?

HYMAN, *hesitates.* I don't know yet. The whole thing is very strange.

> Something darkens Harriet's expression and she be-
> gins to shake her head from side to side and she bursts
> into tears. He comes and puts an arm around her.

HYMAN: What is it?

HARRIET: All her life she did nothing but love everybody!

HYMAN, *reaches out to take her hand.* Harriet.

She looks at him.

What do you want to tell me?

HARRIET: I don't know if it's right to talk about. But of course, it's years and years ago . . .

HYMAN: None of this will ever be repeated; believe me.

HARRIET: Well . . . every first of the year when Uncle Myron was still alive we'd all go down to his basement for a New Year's party. I'm talking like fifteen, sixteen years ago. He's dead now, Myron, but . . . he was . . . you know . . . *Small laugh* . . . a little comical; he always kept this shoebox full of . . . you know, these postcards.

HYMAN: You mean . . .

HARRIET: Yes. French. You know, naked women, and men with these great big . . . you know . . . they hung down like salamis. And everybody'd pass them around and die laughing. It was exactly the same thing every New Year's. But this time, all of a sudden, Phillip . . . they made up after, but . . .

HYMAN: What happened?

HARRIET: Well Sylvia's in the middle of laughing and he grabs the picture out of her hand and gives her a real push up the stairs . . . she got a cut on her scalp. Nobody could believe it, we sat there like he was out of his mind. And

Phillip's impotence

he turns around screaming—I mean, really screaming—
that we're all a bunch of morons and idiots and God
knows what, and marches her up the stairs. I mean it was
just a joke! You know, being it was New Year's Eve and
all . . . *Catches her breath.* I tell you it was months before
anybody'd talk to him again. Because everybody on the
block loves Sylvia.

HYMAN: What do you suppose made him do that?

HARRIET, *shrugs.* . . . Well if you listen to some of the
men—but of course some of the dirty minds on this block
. . . if you spread it over the backyard you'd get tomatoes
six feet high.

HYMAN: Why?—what'd they say?

HARRIET: Well that the reason he got so mad was because
he couldn't . . . you know . . .

HYMAN: Oh really.

HARRIET: . . . anymore. So it made him furious at the pictures. The way he took hold of her—and really *threw* her!
. . . bang! *Gestures violently, her face furious.* It cracked the
banister, I can still hear it.

HYMAN: But they made up.

HARRIET: Listen, to be truthful you have to say it—although
it'll sound crazy . . .

HYMAN: What.

HARRIET: You watch him sometimes when they've got people over and she's talking—he'll sit quietly in the corner, and the expression on that man's face when he's watching her—it could almost break your heart.

HYMAN: Why?

HARRIET: He adores her!

Blackout.

SCENE FOUR

The cellist plays, and is gone.

Stanton Case is getting ready to leave his office. Putting on his blazer and a captain's cap and a foulard. Gellburg enters.

CASE: Good!—you're back. I was just leaving, I wanted to talk to you again about number 611. Sit down for a moment.

Both sit.

We're sailing out through the Narrows in about an hour.

GELLBURG: Beautiful day for it. I'm sorry, I got caught in traffic over in Crown Heights.

CASE: Are you all right? You don't look well.

GELLBURG: Oh no, I'm fine.

CASE: Good. Have you come to anything final on Number 611? I like the price, I can tell you that right off.

GELLBURG: Yes, the price is good, but I'm still . . .

CASE: I've walked past it again; I think with some renovation it would make a fine annex for the Harvard Club.

GELLBURG: It would, it's a very nice structure, yes. I'm not final on it yet but I have a few comments . . . unless you've got to get on the water right away.

CASE: I have a few minutes. Go ahead.

GELLBURG: . . . Before I forget—we got a very nice letter from Jerome.

No reaction from Case.

My boy.

CASE: Oh yes!—how is he doing?

GELLBURG: They're bringing him out to Fort Sill . . . some kind of lecture on artillery.

CASE: Really, now! Well, isn't that nice! . . . Then he's really intending to make a career in the army.

GELLBURG, *surprised Case isn't aware:* Oh absolutely.

CASE: Well that's good, isn't it. It's quite surprising for one of you people—for some reason I'd assumed he just wanted the education.

GELLBURG: Oh no. It's his life. I'll never know how to thank you.

CASE: No trouble at all. The Point can probably use a few of you people to keep the rest of them awake. Now what's this about Number 611?

GELLBURG, *sets himself in all dignity*. You might recall, we used the ABC Plumbing Contractors on a couple of buildings?

CASE: ABC! —I don't recall. What've they got to do with it?

GELLBURG: They're located in the neighborhood, just off Broadway, and on a long shot I went over to see Mr. Liebfreund—he runs ABC. I was wondering if they may have done any work for Wanamaker's.

CASE: Wanamaker's! What's Wanamaker's got to do with it?

GELLBURG: I buy my shirts in Wanamaker's, and last time I was in there I caught my shoe on a splinter sticking up out of the floor.

CASE: Well that store is probably fifty years old.

GELLBURG: Closer to seventy-five. I tripped and almost fell down; this was very remarkable to me, that they would leave a floor in such condition. So I began wondering about it—

CASE: About what?

GELLBURG: Number 611 is two blocks from Wanamaker's. *A little extra-wise grin.* They're the biggest business in the area, a whole square block, after all. Anyway, sure enough, turns out ABC does all Wanamaker's plumbing work. And Liebfreund tells me he's had to keep patching up their boilers *because they canceled installation of new boilers last winter.* A permanent cancellation.

Pause.

CASE: And what do you make of that?

GELLBURG: I think it means they're either moving the store, or maybe going out of business.

CASE: *Wanamaker's?*

GELLBURG: It's possible, I understand the family is practically died out. Either way, if Wanamaker's disappears, Mr. Case, that neighborhood in my opinion is no longer prime.

CASE: Then what are you telling me?

GELLBURG: I would not touch Number 611 with a ten-foot pole. If that neighborhood starts to slide, Number 611 is a great big slice of lemon.

CASE: Well. That's very disappointing. It would have made a wonderful club annex.

GELLBURG: With a thing like the Harvard Club you have got to think of the far distant future, Mr. Case, I don't have to tell you that, and the future of that part of Broadway is a definite possible negative. *Raising a monitory finger:* I emphasize "possible," mind you; only God can predict.

CASE: Well I must say, I would never have thought of Wanamaker's disappearing. You've been more than thorough, Gellburg, we appreciate it. I've got to run now, but we'll talk about this further . . . *Glances at his watch.* Mustn't miss the tide . . . *Moves, indicates.* Take a brandy if you like. Wife all right?

GELLBURG: Oh yes, she's fine!

CASE, *the faint shadow of a warning:* Sure everything's all right with you—we don't want you getting sick now.

GELLBURG: Oh no, I'm very well, very well.

CASE: I'll be back on Monday, we'll go into this further. *Indicates.* Take a brandy if you like.

GELLBURG: Yes, sir, I might!

> *Case exits rather jauntily. Gellburg stands alone; his hands come up and cover his suffering face.*

> *Blackout.*

SCENE FIVE

The cello plays, and the music falls away.

Sylvia in bed, reading a book. She looks up as Hyman enters. He is in his riding clothes. A certain excitement at seeing him.

SYLVIA: Oh, doctor!

HYMAN: I let myself in, hope I didn't scare you . . .

SYLVIA: Oh no, I'm glad. Sit down. You been riding?

HYMAN: Yes. All the way down to Brighton Beach, nice long ride.

SYLVIA: You don't say! How many miles is that?

HYMAN: About six, there and back.

SYLVIA: You really love doing that, don't you.

HYMAN: Well there's no telephone on a horse.

She laughs.

Ocean Parkway is like a German forest this time of the morning—riding under that archway of maple trees is like poetry.

SYLVIA: Wonderful. I never did anything like that.

HYMAN: Well get better and I'll take you out and teach you sometime. So how's it going today, did you try the exercise?

SYLVIA: I can't do it.

HYMAN, *shaking a finger at her:* You've *got* to do it, Sylvia. Let's have a look.

> *He sits on the bed and draws the cover off her legs, then raises her nightgown. She inhales with a certain anticipation as he does so. He feels her toes.*

You feel this at all?

SYLVIA: Well . . . not really.

HYMAN: I'm going to pinch your toe. Ready?

SYLVIA: All right.

> *He pinches her big toe sharply; she doesn't react. He rests a palm on her leg.*

HYMAN: Your skin feels a little too cool. You're going to lose your muscle tone if you don't move. Your legs will begin to lose volume and shrink . . .

SYLVIA, *tears threaten.* I know . . . !

HYMAN: And you have such beautiful legs, Sylvia. I'm afraid you're getting comfortable in this condition . . .

SYLVIA: I'm not. I keep trying to move them . . .

HYMAN: But look now—here it's eleven in the morning and you're happily tucked into bed like it's midnight.

SYLVIA: But I've tried . . . !

HYMAN: Sylvia, dear, you have a strong beautiful body . . .

SYLVIA: But what can I do, I can't feel anything!

> *She sits up with her face raised to him; he starts to* *cup it in his hand, but stands and moves abruptly* *away. Then turning back to her . . .*

HYMAN: I really should find someone else for you.

SYLVIA: Why!—I don't want anyone else!

HYMAN: I'm beginning to feel afraid of myself with you.

SYLVIA, *pleased and surprised:* With *me?*

HYMAN: You're a very attractive woman, don't you know that?

SYLVIA, *deeply excited, glancing away shyly:* . . . Well, you mustn't get anyone else.

HYMAN, *he comes and sits on the bed.* I can't help it, the sight of you fills me up with pity. —I won't talk to you again like this, but just being near you makes me very happy . . .

> *Her eyes fill with tears and she covers her face. He touches her hair.*

Tell me the truth, Sylvia. Sylvia?

> *She lowers her hands and faces him.*

How did this happen to you?

SYLVIA, *she avoids his gaze.* I don't know.

HYMAN: You have no idea at all?

> *Sylvia shakes her head, silent.*

HYMAN: I think you wish you could tell me something, don't you. —You mustn't feel ashamed. I'll never tell anyone.

SYLVIA: . . . I like you. . . . A lot.

HYMAN, *grins*. Well what's wrong with that?

SYLVIA: Nothing. *Relieved; a fresher mood:* —Harriet says you used to take out our cousin Roslyn Fein.

HYMAN: It's possible, I don't remember.

SYLVIA: Well you had so many, didn't you.

HYMAN: When I was younger.

SYLVIA: Roslyn said you used to do acrobatics on the beach? And all the girls would stand around going crazy for you.

HYMAN: That's a long time ago. . . .

SYLVIA: And you'd take them under the boardwalk. *Laughs.*

HYMAN: Nobody had money for anything else. Didn't you use to go to the beach?

SYLVIA: Sure. But I never did anything like that.

HYMAN: You must have been very shy.

SYLVIA: I was the oldest. I had to look out for my sisters. But I guess I was shy, too.

HYMAN: Is that why you can't tell me?

SYLVIA: I don't know how this happened, I swear.

HYMAN: You have no suspicion? Come, let's try to imagine a reason. Whatever comes to your mind. Come on.

SYLVIA: I don't know! Couldn't we talk about other things?

HYMAN: All right. *Picks up a book on the bed.* What's this?

SYLVIA: *Anthony Adverse.*

HYMAN: Oh yes, I read they've sold a million copies.

SYLVIA: I rent it from Womrath's. It's wonderful.

HYMAN, *sets the book down.* Tell me from your heart—

SYLVIA: I can't. *She catches a sob.*

HYMAN: Are you afraid right now?

SYLVIA: Not now.

HYMAN: Most of the time?

SYLVIA: No, not . . . *A hesitation.* Yes.

HYMAN: We must get you out of this.

SYLVIA: I'm trying!

HYMAN: Talk about yourself, was Phillip your first boy-friend?

SYLVIA: The first serious.

HYMAN: He's a fine man.

SYLVIA: Yes, he is.

HYMAN: Is he interesting to be with?

SYLVIA: Interesting?

HYMAN: Do you have things to talk about?

SYLVIA: Well . . . business, mostly. I was head bookkeeper for Empire Steel in Long Island City . . . years ago, when we met, I mean.

HYMAN: He didn't want you to work?

SYLVIA: No.

HYMAN: I imagine you were a good businesswoman.

SYLVIA: Oh, I loved it! I've always enjoyed . . . you know, people depending on me.

HYMAN: Yes. —Do I frighten you, talking like this?

SYLVIA: A little. —But I want you to.

HYMAN: Why?

SYLVIA: I don't know. You make me feel . . . hopeful.

HYMAN: You mean of getting better?

SYLVIA: —Of myself. Of getting . . . *Breaks off.*

HYMAN: Getting what?

> *She shakes her head, refusing to go on.*

. . . Free?

> *She suddenly kisses the palm of his hand. He wipes her hair away from her eyes. He stands up and walks a few steps away.*

HYMAN: I want you to raise your knees.

> *She doesn't move.*

Come, bring up your knees.

SYLVIA, *she tries.* I can't!

HYMAN: You can. I want you to send your thoughts into your hips. Tense your hips. Think of the bones in your hips. Come on now. The strongest muscles in your body are right there, you still have tremendous power there. Tense your hips.

> *She is tensing.*

Now tense your thighs. Those are long dense muscles with tremendous power. Do it, draw up your knees. Come on, raise your knees.

With an exhaled gasp she gives up. Remaining yards away . . .

Sylvia, dear, listen to me . . . I haven't been this moved by a woman in a very long time.

SYLVIA, *covering her face:* Oh, my God!

HYMAN: Your body strength must be marvelous. The depth of your flesh must be wonderful. Why are you cut off from yourself? You should be dancing, you should be stretching out in the sun. . . . Sylvia, I know you know more than you're saying, why can't you open up to me? Speak to me. Sylvia? Say anything.

She looks at him in silence.

I promise I won't tell a soul. What is in your mind right now?

A pause.

SYLVIA: Tell me about Germany.

HYMAN, *surprised:* Germany. Why Germany?

SYLVIA: Why did you go there to study?

HYMAN: The American medical schools have quotas on Jews, I would have had to wait for years and maybe never get in.

SYLVIA: But they hate Jews there, don't they?

HYMAN: These Nazis can't possibly last, dear— Why are you so preoccupied with them?

SYLVIA: When I saw that picture in the *Times*—they showed two old men with beards . . .

HYMAN: But that was a staged demonstration—to work up the people against Jews. It's like we have Ku Klux Klan parades, but you know most Americans aren't like them.

SYLVIA, *as though suspended in air:* . . . Yes.

HYMAN: There's something else, isn't there?

She is lost in thought.

Sylvia?

SYLVIA: I can't talk about it.

HYMAN: Dear Sylvia, do you want to be permanently crippled?

She shakes her head.

You must talk about it; this is not going to go away by itself! *He walks and turns.* I'll stand over here, and I want you to raise your left knee. Go on, try it. Just concentrate on your left knee.

She seems to be trying.

Keep it up, concentrate, raise it. Do it for me.

But she relaxes, defeated.

Sylvia. Look at me, please.

She turns to him from the pillow.

Is it Phillip?

She turns her face away.

Listen. I want you to imagine something.

She turns to him, curious.

I want you to imagine that we've made love.

Startled, she laughs tensely. He joins this laugh.

I've made love to you. And now it's over and we are lying together. And you begin to tell me some secret things. Things that are way down deep on your heart. *Slight pause.* Sylvia, dear—tell me about Phillip.

He returns to the bed, bends and kisses her. She is silent, does not grasp his head to hold him. He straightens up.

Think about it. We'll talk tomorrow again. Okay?

He exits. She lies there inert for a moment. Then she tenses with effort, trying to raise her knee. It doesn't work. She reaches down and lifts the knee, and then the other, and lies there that way. Then she lets her knees spread apart . . .

Blackout.

Act Two

SCENE ONE

The cellist plays, disappears.

Hyman's office. Gellburg enters, sits. Immediately Margaret follows him in with a cup of cocoa and hands it to him.

GELLBURG: Cocoa?

MARGARET: I drink a lot of it, it calms the nerves. Have you lost weight?

GELLBURG, *impatience with her prying:* A little, I think.

MARGARET: Did you always sigh so much?

GELLBURG: Sigh?

MARGARET: You probably don't realize you're doing it. You should have him listen to your heart.

GELLBURG: No–no, I think I'm all right. *Sighs.* I guess I've always sighed. Is that a sign of something?

MARGARET: Not necessarily; but ask Harry. He's just finishing with a patient, he'll be right with you. —There's no change, I understand.

GELLBURG: No, she's the same. *Impatiently hands her the cup.* I can't drink this.

MARGARET: Are you eating at all?

GELLBURG, *suddenly shifting his mode:* I came to talk to *him.*

MARGARET, *sharply:* I was just trying to be helpful!

GELLBURG: I'm kind of upset, I didn't mean any . . .

> *Hyman enters, surprising her. She exits, insulted.*
> *Hyman angrily watches her go.*

HYMAN: I'm sorry. But she means well.

> *Gellburg silently nods, irritation intact.*

HYMAN: It won't happen again. *He takes his seat.* I have to admit, though, she has a very good diagnostic sense. Women are more instinctive sometimes . . .

GELLBURG: Excuse me, I don't come here to be talking to her.

HYMAN: Come on, Phillip, take it easy. I said it won't happen again. What's Sylvia doing?

GELLBURG, *it takes him a moment to compose himself.* I don't know . . . I don't know what she's doing.

> *Hyman waits. Gellburg has a tortured look; now he seems to brace himself, and faces the doctor with what seems a haughty air.*

I decided to try to do what you advised. —About showing her more love.

HYMAN: . . . Yes?

GELLBURG: So I decided to try to do it with her.

HYMAN: . . . Sex?

GELLBURG: What then, handball? Of course sex.

> *The openness of this hostility mystifies Hyman, who becomes apologetic.*

HYMAN: Phillip, I'm only trying to get things clear—you mean you've done it or you're going to?

GELLBURG, *long pause; he seems not to be sure he wants to continue. Now he sounds reasonable again:* You see, we haven't been really . . . together. For . . . quite a long time. *Correcting:* Specially since this started to happen.

HYMAN: Yes. You mean the last two weeks.

GELLBURG: Well yes. *Great discomfort.* And some time before that.

HYMAN: I see. *But he desists from asking how long a time before that. A pause.*

GELLBURG: So I thought maybe it would help her if . . . you know.

HYMAN: Yes, I think the warmth would help. That's correct.

GELLBURG, *an inner floundering for a moment:* Yes.

HYMAN: In fact, to be candid, Phillip—you want me to be straight out with you, right?

GELLBURG: Yes, sure.

HYMAN: I'm beginning to wonder if this whole fear of the Nazis isn't because she feels . . . extremely vulnerable; I mean in some radical way. I think of it like in a dream, where you're about to get killed and you can't move, you know what I mean? I'm not blaming you, Phillip, but . . . a woman who doesn't feel loved can get very lost, you know? —Something wrong? *He has noticed a strangeness.*

GELLBURG: Why shouldn't she feel loved? I love her.

HYMAN: I know that . . .

GELLBURG: She says she's not being loved?

HYMAN: Oh no. I'm talking about how she may feel.

GELLBURG: Listen . . . *Struggles for a moment.* I have something on my mind that I . . . *Breaks off. Now, firmly* . . . I'm wondering if you could put me in touch with somebody.

HYMAN: You mean for yourself?

GELLBURG: I don't know; I'm not sure what they do, though.

HYMAN: —You just talk things out with them if there's something disturbing you. I know a very good man at the hospital, if you want me to set it up.

GELLBURG: Well maybe not yet, let me let you know.

HYMAN: Sure. *Short pause.* Has something happened?

GELLBURG: Your wife says I sigh a lot. Does that mean something?

HYMAN: Could just be tension. Come in when you have a little time, I'll look you over. What's happened?

GELLBURG, *a brief struggle with himself.* I don't know the woman anymore. She's a total stranger.

HYMAN: Why?

GELLBURG: I was late last night—I had to be in Jersey all afternoon, a problem we have there—she was sound asleep. So I made myself some spaghetti. Usually she puts something out for me.

HYMAN: She has no problem cooking.

GELLBURG: I told you—she gets around the kitchen fine in the wheelchair. Flora shops in the morning—that's the maid. Although I'm beginning to wonder if she gets out and walks around when I leave the house.

HYMAN: Sylvia? —You serious?

GELLBURG, *a grin.* You know this whole thing is against me.

HYMAN, *alarmed:* Oh now wait, Phillip . . .

GELLBURG: She knows what she's doing, Hyman, you're not blind.

HYMAN: We've stuck needles into her skin with no pain reaction. . . . That'd be pretty hard to fake. It's impossible. —She is paralyzed, Phillip, it's not a trick—she's suffering.

GELLBURG, *a sideways glance at Hyman:* What do you talk about when you see her?

HYMAN, *shrugs, mimimizing:* I talk about getting her to walk, that's all. Why?

GELLBURG: What does she say about me?

HYMAN: Very little, to tell you the truth.

GELLBURG: Does she have any idea what this is doing to me?

HYMAN: She feels a great obligation to you, Phillip, that woman cares about you, believe me. This thing is not against you; she's just helpless.

GELLBURG, *he seems momentarily on the edge of being reassured and studies Hyman's face for a moment, nodding very slightly.* You know, she talks like you see right through her.

HYMAN: I wish I could.

GELLBURG: She believes in you a lot. What do you talk about with her?

HYMAN: I've told you that, Phillip; I don't know what you're driving at. You're taking a wrong attitude . . .

GELLBURG, *sharply:* Please don't tell me what attitude to take.

Silence.

HYMAN: Look, if you don't trust me . . .

GELLBURG: I do trust you. I would never believe I could talk this way to another person.

Pause.

HYMAN: What's been happening, can you tell me?

Gellburg is still locked into himself.

GELLBURG, *quite suddenly seems about to break up:* I can't bear what's happening to her.

HYMAN: I know what you're going through, I sympathize with you.

GELLBURG: I don't know where I am anymore. I sleep an hour a night, tossing and turning. *Sighs, seems out of breath.*

HYMAN: I wish you'd tell me what's on your mind, can you? And you know it stays in this office.

GELLBURG: The first time we talked you asked me if we . . . how many times a week.

HYMAN: Yes.

GELLBURG: Why did you ask that?

HYMAN: Well as I explained, there's usually a sexual element in this kind of hysteria.

GELLBURG, *nods*. . . . I have a problem sometimes.

HYMAN: Yes?

GELLBURG: Yes.

HYMAN: Well that's fairly common, you know.

GELLBURG, *relieved:* You see it often?

HYMAN: Oh very often, yes.

GELLBURG, *a tense challenging smile:* Ever happen to you?

HYMAN, *surprised:* . . . Me? Well sure, a few times. Is this something recent?

GELLBURG: Well . . . yes. Recent and also . . . *Breaks off, indicating the past with a gesture of his hand.*

HYMAN: I see. It doesn't help if you're under tension, you know.

GELLBURG: That's right.

HYMAN: Just try to avoid thinking it's the end of the world, because it's not—you're still a young man. Think of it like the ocean—it goes out but it always comes in again.

But the thing to keep in mind is that she loves you and
wants you.

Gellburg looks wide-eyed.

You know that, don't you?

GELLBURG, *silently nods for an instant.* My sister-in-law Harriet says you were a real hotshot on the beach years ago.

HYMAN: Years ago, yes.

GELLBURG: I used to wonder if it's because Sylvia's the only
one I was ever with.

HYMAN: Why would that matter?

GELLBURG: I don't know exactly—it used to prey on my
mind that . . . you know, maybe she expected more.

HYMAN: That's a common idea, Phillip.

GELLBURG: It is?

HYMAN: No matter how many women you've been with.

GELLBURG: Is that true?

HYMAN: In fact, some men take on a lot of women not out
of confidence but because they're afraid to lose it.

GELLBURG, *fascinated:* Huh! I'd never of thought of that. —A doctor must get a lot of peculiar cases, I bet.

HYMAN: Everybody's peculiar in one way or another. Why don't you try to tell me what happened . . . if you'd like to.

GELLBURG: All right . . . *Sighs.* I get into bed. She's sound asleep . . . *Breaks off. Resumes.* Nothing like it ever happened to me, I got a . . . a big yen for her. She's even more beautiful when she sleeps. I gave her a kiss. On the mouth. She didn't wake up. I never had such a yen in my life.

Long pause.

HYMAN: And?

Gellburg silent.

Did you do it?

GELLBURG: . . . Yes.

HYMAN, *he notes something confusingly tentative in Gellburg.* . . . How did she react? —It's been some time since you did it, you say.

GELLBURG: Well yes.

HYMAN: Then what was the reaction?

GELLBURG: She was . . . *Searches for the word* . . . gasping. I
thought of what you told me—about loving her now; I
felt I'd brought her out of it. I was almost sure of it. She
was like a different woman than I ever knew.

HYMAN: That's wonderful. Did she move her legs?

GELLBURG, *unprepared for that question:* . . . I . . . think so.

HYMAN: Well did she or didn't she?

GELLBURG: Well I was so excited I didn't really notice, but
I guess she must have.

HYMAN: That's wonderful, why are you so upset?

GELLBURG: Well let me finish, there's more to it.

HYMAN: Sorry, go ahead.

GELLBURG: —I brought her some breakfast this morning
and—you know—started to—you know—talk a little
about it. She looked at me like I was crazy. She claims
she doesn't remember doing it. It never happened.

> *Hyman is silent, plays with a pen. Something eva-
> sive in this.*

How could she not remember it?

HYMAN: You're sure she was awake?

GELLBURG: How could she not be?

HYMAN: Did she say anything during the . . . ?

GELLBURG: Well no, but she's never said much.

HYMAN: Did she open her eyes?

GELLBURG: I'm not sure. We were in the dark, but she usually keeps them closed. *Impatiently:* But she was . . . she was groaning, panting . . . she had to be awake! And now to say she doesn't remember?

Shaken, Hyman gets up and moves; a pause.

HYMAN: So what do you think is behind it?

GELLBURG: Well what would any man think?

HYMAN: You mean she's . . .

GELLBURG: She's trying to turn me into nothing!

HYMAN: Now wait, you're jumping to conclusions.

GELLBURG: Is such a thing possible? I want your medical opinion—could a woman not remember?

HYMAN, *a moment, then:* . . . How did she look when she said that; did she seem sincere about not remembering?

GELLBURG: She looked like I was talking about something on the moon. Finally, she said a terrible thing. I still can't get over it.

HYMAN: What'd she say?

GELLBURG: That I'd imagined doing it.

Long pause. Hyman doesn't move.

What's your opinion?

HYMAN: About what?

GELLBURG: Well . . . could a man imagine such a thing? Is that possible?

HYMAN, *after a moment:* Tell you what; supposing I have another talk with her and see what I can figure out?

GELLBURG, *angrily demanding:* You have an opinion, don't you?—How could a man imagine such a thing!

HYMAN: I don't know what to say . . .

GELLBURG: What do you mean you don't know what to say! It's impossible, isn't it? To invent such a thing?

HYMAN, *fear of being out of his depth:* Phillip, don't cross-examine me, I'm doing everythig I know to help you!

—Frankly, I can't follow what you're telling me—you're sure in your own mind you had relations with her?

GELLBURG: How can you even ask me such a thing? If I wasn't sure would I say it? *Stands.* I don't understand you.

HYMAN: What's there to understand?

GELLBURG, *shaking with fear and anger:* I don't understand your attitude! *He starts out.*

HYMAN: Phillip, please! *In fear he intercepts Gellburg.* What attitude, what are you talking about?

GELLBURG: I'm going to vomit, I swear—I don't feel well . . .

HYMAN: What happened . . . has she said something about me?

GELLBURG: What do you mean? What could she say?

HYMAN, *shouting:* I don't understand why you're so upset with me!

GELLBURG, *shouts:* What are you doing!

HYMAN, *guiltily:* What am *I* doing! What are you talking about!

GELLBURG: She is trying to destroy me! And you stand there! And what do you do! Are you a doctor or what! *He goes right up to Hyman's face.* Why don't you give me a straight answer about anything! Everything is in-and-out and around-the-block! —Listen, I've made up my mind; I don't want you seeing her anymore.

HYMAN: I think she's the one has to decide that.

PHILLIP: I am deciding it! It's decided!

> *He storms out. Hyman stands there, guilty, alarmed.*
> *Margaret enters.*

MARGARET: Now what? He gone off too? *Seeing his anxiety:* Why are you looking like that?

> *He looks at her in silence, and evasively returns to*
> *his desk chair.*

Are *you* in trouble?

HYMAN: Me! Cut it out, will you?

MARGARET: Cut what out? I asked a question—are you?

HYMAN: I said to cut it out, Margaret!

> *Silence. Then . . .*

MARGARET: I will never understand it. Except I do, I guess; you believe women. Woman tells you the earth is flat and for that five minutes you're swept away, helpless.

HYMAN, *laughs:* Nothing's happened. *Nothing has happened!* Why are you going on about it!

MARGARET: I'm not talking like this because I gained some weight. You just don't realize how transparent you are. You're a pane of glass, Harry— Mrs. Gellburg has you by the short ones . . .

HYMAN: You know what baffles me?

MARGARET: . . . And it's irritating. What is it—just new ass all the time? But what can be new about an ass?

HYMAN: There's been nobody for at least five years . . . more!—maybe six, seven! I can't remember anymore!

MARGARET: What baffles you?

HYMAN: Why I take your suspicions seriously.

MARGARET: Oh that's easy. —You love the truth.

HYMAN, *a deep sigh, facing upward:* I'm exhausted.

MARGARET: What about asking Charley Whitman to see her?

HYMAN: She's frightened to death of psychiatry, she thinks it means she's crazy.

MARGARET: Well, she is, in a way, isn't she?

HYMAN: I don't see it that way at all.

MARGARET: Getting this hysterical about something on the other side of the world is sane?

HYMAN: When she talks about it, it's not the other side of the world, it's on the next block.

MARGARET: And that's sane?

HYMAN: I don't know what it is! I just get the feeling sometimes that she *knows* something, something that . . . It's like she's connected to some . . . some wire that goes half around the world, some truth that other people are blind to . . .

MARGARET: I think you've got to get somebody on this who won't be carried away, Harry.

HYMAN: I am not carried away!

MARGARET: You really believe that Sylvia Gellburg is being threatened by these Nazis? Is that real or is it hysterical?

HYMAN: So call it hysterical, does that bring you one inch closer to what is driving that woman? It's not a word that's driving her, Margaret—she *knows* something! I don't know what it is, and she may not either—but I tell you it's real.

A moment.

MARGARET: What an interesting life you have, Harry.

Blackout.

SCENE TWO

Later. Hyman's office. Harriet is seated. Hyman is writing a prescription, hands it to her.

HYMAN: Take one before bed and let me know how you feel in a day or two.

HARRIET: It's like I can't take a really full breath. I know what it is, I'm so worried about my sister.

HYMAN: I understand, but your heart is fine. Be sure to give her my best. *Stands to dismiss her.*

HARRIET, *with embarrassment:* I haven't finished about her.

HYMAN: Oh. *He sits again.*

HARRIET: I don't know how to say it. I've never seen her act like this.

HYMAN: How?

HARRIET: She wants you to come and see her . . . you know, more often.

HYMAN: I'll try to stop by tomorrow . . .

> *It's impossible to proceed, she nervously studies her hands.*

Well what is it?

HARRIET: She's afraid you might get her another doctor because of Phillip.

HYMAN: Certainly not if she doesn't want me to . . .

HARRIET: . . . She loves you, doctor. I'm not kidding.

HYMAN, *affected, but trying to make light of it:* Well that's very nice of her but we're two married people.

HARRIET, *half giggling, half desperate:* I'm serious. You mustn't leave her. I think she's afraid of Phillip.

HYMAN: What do you mean, afraid?

HARRIET: She said to ask you to come tonight. This is his night to be in Jersey till late; there's some zoning thing he has to be at. I promised to tell you. Honestly, she's like in a fever.

HYMAN: It's impossible, I couldn't be making evening visits under these circumstances.

HARRIET: Why not? You've gone there five or six times . . .

HYMAN: Yes, but not . . . not under these circumstances. I want you to go back and tell her that she mustn't let herself be frightened by Phillip.

Margaret enters.

MARGARET: The natives are getting restless out there.

HYMAN: I'll be right out . . .

MARGARET: Mrs. Kaplan is . . .

HYMAN, *suppressing a shout:* I will be right out, Margaret!

> *She is taken aback; glances at Harriet, trying to figure what this is about. Then turns and exits angrily.*

Go now. And tell her she can call me anytime.

HARRIET: She says that when you sit on the bed and talk with her . . . that she can feel the strength starting to come back into her body.

HYMAN, *vanity and fear:* Okay, Harriet, thank you. *He presses her toward the exit.*

Margaret enters.

MARGARET: Mrs. Kaplan's leaving.

HARRIET: You won't give up on her, will you?

HYMAN: No-no, of couse not . . . good-bye now.

HARRIET, *to Margaret:* He's so wonderful!

Harriet exits.

MARGARET, *Hyman glances at her, speechless:* I am not going through this one more time, Harry! What is going on with that woman!

HYMAN: . . . I'm getting scared.

MARGARET, *struck; touches his cheek:* My god, look at you, you're pale.

HYMAN: I have a terrible feeling. Try to be helpful, will you?

MARGARET: You're going to drive me crazy.

HYMAN: God, why did I ever get into this!

Blackout.

SCENE THREE

The cellist plays, music fades away.

Stanton Case is standing with hands clasped behind his back as though staring out a window. A dark mood. Gellburg enters behind him but he doesn't turn at once.

GELLBURG: Excuse me . . .

CASE, *turns:* Oh, good morning. You wanted to see me.

GELLBURG: If you have a minute I'd appreciate . . .

CASE, *as he sits:* —You don't look well, are you all right?

GELLBURG: Oh I'm fine, maybe a cold coming on . . .

Since he hasn't been invited to sit he glances at a chair then back at Case, who still leaves him hanging—and he sits on the chair's edge.

I wanted you to know how bad I feel about 611 Broadway. I'm very sorry.

CASE: Yes. Well. So it goes, I guess.

GELLBURG: I know how you had your heart set on it and I
   . . . I tell you the news knocked me over; they gave no
   sign they were talking to Allan Kershowitz or anybody
   else . . .

CASE: It's very disappointing—in fact, I'd already begun talking to an architect friend about renovations.

GELLBURG: Really. Well, I can't tell you how . . .

CASE: I'd gotten a real affection for that building. It certainly
   would have made a perfect annex. And probably a great
   investment too.

GELLBURG: Well, not necessarily, if Wanamakers ever pulls
   out.

CASE: . . . Yes, about Wanamakers—I should tell you—
   when I found out that Kershowitz had outbid us I was
   flabbergasted after what you'd said about the neighborhood going downhill once the store was gone— Kershowitz is no fool, I need hardly say. So I mentioned it
   to one of our club members who I know is related to a
   member of the Wanamaker board. —He tells me there
   has never been any discussion whatever about the company moving out; he was simply amazed at the idea.

GELLBURG: But the man at ABC . . .

CASE, *impatience showing:* ABC lost their boiler work because Wanamakers changed to another contractor three years ago. It had nothing to do with the store moving out. Nothing.

GELLBURG: . . . I don't know what to say, I . . . I just . . . I'm awfully sorry . . .

CASE: Well, it's a beautiful building, let's hope Kershowitz puts it to some worthwhile use. —You have any idea what he plans to do with it?

GELLBURG: Me? Oh no, I don't really know Kershowitz.

CASE: Oh! I thought you said you knew him for years?

GELLBURG: . . . Well, I "know" him, but not . . . we're not personal friends or anything, we just met at closings a few times, and things like that. And maybe once or twice in restaurants, I think, but . . .

CASE: I see. I guess I misunderstood, I thought you were fairly close.

> *Case says no more; the full stop shoots Gellburg's anxiety way up.*

GELLBURG: I hope you're not . . . I mean I never mentioned to Kershowitz that you were interested in 611.

CASE: Mentioned? What do you mean?

GELLBURG: Nothing; just that . . . it almost sounds like I had something to do with him grabbing the building away from under you.

CASE: Oh.

GELLBURG: I would never do a thing like that to you! I hope you're not . . .

CASE: I didn't say that, did I. If I seem upset it's being screwed out of that building, and by a man whose methods I've never particularly admired.

GELLBURG: Yes. Well . . . *stands* . . . I can't tell you how sorry I am, but . . .

Breaks off into silence.

CASE: I'm not clear about what you wanted to say to me, or have I missed some . . . ?

GELLBURG: No no, I ah . . . just what I've said.

CASE, *his mystification peaking:* What's the matter with you? What is happening?

Blackout.

The cello plays its tune.

Sylvia in a wheelchair is listening to Eddie Cantor on the radio, singing "If You Knew Susie Like I Know Susie." She has an amused look, taps a finger to the rhythm. Her bed is nearby, on it a folded newspaper.

Hyman appears. She instantly smiles, turns off the radio, and holds a hand out to him. He comes and shakes hands.

SYLVIA, *indicating the radio:* I simply can't stand Eddie Cantor, can you?

HYMAN: Cut it out now, I heard you laughing halfway up the stairs.

SYLVIA: I know, but I can't stand him. This Crosby is the one I like. You ever hear him?

HYMAN: I can't stand these crooners—they're making ten, twenty thousand dollars a week and never spent a day in medical school. *She laughs.* Anyway, I'm an opera man.

opera = church

SYLVIA: I never saw an opera. They must be hard to understand, I bet.

HYMAN: Nothing to understand—either she wants to and
he doesn't or he wants to and she doesn't. *She laughs.*
Either way one of them gets killed and the other one
jumps off a building.

SYLVIA: Honestly?

HYMAN: You go for the music—it's like the church or the
synagogue—who understands Latin or Hebrew? But it
makes them feel good anyway.

SYLVIA: I'm so glad you could come.

HYMAN, *settling into chair near the bed:* You ready? I want to
ask you a question.

SYLVIA: Phillip had to go to Jersey for a zoning meeting . . .

HYMAN: Just as well, it's a question for you.

SYLVIA: . . . There's some factory the firm owns there . . .

HYMAN: Come on, dear, don't be nervous.

SYLVIA: What's the question?

HYMAN: I warn you, it's very personal, okay?

SYLVIA, *excited:* Oh! . . . Well, sure. *Laughs.* How personal?

HYMAN: Personal as you can get.

SYLVIA, *blushing but game:* Oh! . . . Okay.

HYMAN: You seem more rested.

SYLVIA: I slept a little better, but I'm worried about Phillip. I've never seen him look so unhappy.

HYMAN: What does he say?

SYLVIA, *shrugs.* He never tells me his troubles.

HYMAN: Have you tried the exercises?

SYLVIA: It's impossible . . . My back aches, will you help me onto the bed?

HYMAN: Sure.

> *She grips him around the shoulders.*

There we go.

> *And he swings her onto the bed and she lies back.*
> *He leaves the bedside.*

What's that perfume?

SYLVIA: Harriet found it in my drawer. I think Jerome bought it for one of my birthdays years ago. It's nice, isn't it.

HYMAN: Lovely. Your hair is different.

SYLVIA: Or maybe it was Phillip. *Puffs up her hair.* Harriet did it; she's loved playing with my hair since we were kids. *Patting the mattress:* Will you sit here so I don't have to turn?

With the slightest hesitation he comes to her and sits on the bed. She wants to chat.

Did you hear all those birds this morning?

HYMAN: Amazing, yes; a whole cloud . . . hundreds of them. They shot up like a spray in front of my horse.

SYLVIA, *partially to keep him:* You know, as a child, when we first moved here there were so many birds and rabbits and even foxes.

HYMAN: In Coney Island we used to kill rabbits with slingshots.

SYLVIA, *wrinkling her nose in disgust:* Why!

HYMAN: To see if we could. It was heaven for kids.

SYLVIA: I know! The nearest grocery was miles away over on Church Avenue, so we'd buy potatoes in fifty-pound sacks. And women baked bread and put up jellies and tomatoes from the garden.

HYMAN: Remember the Italians planting all the empty lots with tomatoes and peppers?

SYLVIA: Oh yes! And their old grandmas, coming out to pick weeds for salad.

HYMAN: And dandelion wine.

SYLVIA: Brooklyn was really beautiful, wasn't it? I think people were happier then. My mother could stand on our porch and watch us all the way to school right across the open fields for—must have been a mile. *A little laugh.* And I would tie a clothesline around my three sisters so I wouldn't have to keep chasing after them!

HYMAN: You always had all the responsibility.

SYLVIA: Well, I was the oldest. —I'm so glad—honestly . . . *A cozy little laugh.* I feel good every time you come.

HYMAN: I've been discussing your situation with a man in my hospital—a friend of mine. —A psychiatrist.

SYLVIA, *with quick alarm:* Oh no, please—he wouldn't know me the way you do . . . And what will it cost? Phillip will never allow . . .

HYMAN: Now Sylvia, this has to be faced.

SYLVIA: But I'm not crazy, am I?

HYMAN: Now listen to me; I've learned that these kinds of symptoms come from very deep in the mind. I am not trained for that. A doctor would have to deal with your dreams to get any results, your deepest secret feelings, you understand?

SYLVIA: But when you talk to me I really feel my strength starting to come back . . .

HYMAN: I don't think that will do it, dear. And meantime I worry about your legs weakening. In fact, you should already be having therapy to keep up your circulation.

A change in her expression, a sudden inwardness which he notices.

You have a long life ahead of you, you don't want to live it in a wheelchair, do you?

SYLVIA: But why couldn't I tell my dreams to you?

HYMAN: I'm not trained to . . .

SYLVIA: I'd like to tell you, can I? I have the same one every night just as I'm falling asleep.

HYMAN: Well . . . all right, what is it?

SYLVIA: I'm in a street. Everything is sort of gray. And there's a crowd of people. —You won't mention this?

HYMAN: Of course not.

SYLVIA: People packed in all around, but they're looking for me. And then I slowly realize who they are.

HYMAN: Who are they?

SYLVIA: They're Germans. And I begin to run away. And the whole crowd is chasing after me. Then just as I'm escaping around a corner a man catches me and pushes me down and gets on top of me and begins kissing me, and then he starts to cut off my breast. And he raises himself up and . . . I think it's Phillip.

Pause.

HYMAN: You poor woman. I suppose the crowd must be from the newspapers you're reading.

SYLVIA: I know, it was just like that picture with those old men scrubbing the sidewalk. But how could Phillip be like . . . he was almost like one of the others?

HYMAN: The Germans.

SYLVIA: Yes.

HYMAN: I don't know. Why do you think?

SYLVIA: Would it be possible . . . because Phillip . . . I mean
. . . *A little laugh* . . . he sounds sometimes like he doesn't
like Jews? *Correcting:* Of course he doesn't *mean* it, but
maybe in my mind it's like he's . . . *Breaks off.*

HYMAN, *he has the same thought; a note of alarm has crept into
his voice:* . . . Sylvia, dear, you simply have to let me call
this other man . . .

SYLVIA: But I'd be embarrassed to tell anybody else.

HYMAN: Why? There's nothing shameful in a dream like
that.

SYLVIA: . . . There are other things.

HYMAN: Oh. —You'll see this man, all right?

SYLVIA, *she grasps his hand.* You're not leaving now, are you?

HYMAN: In a few minutes. I'm sure you'd like this doctor,
can I call him tomorrow?

SYLVIA, *her breath is coming deeper; a frantic urgency begins in her:* Couldn't you stay till Phillip comes? It can't be more than half an hour or so . . .

HYMAN: . . . Is something frightening you?

> *She is silent, turns away.*

Sylvia?

> *He tries to turn her face to him, but she resists.*

What is it?

> *She is unable to speak.*

Not Phillip, is it?

> *She turns to him, the answer in her eyes. He is amazed.*

I see.

> *He stands, moves from the bed and halts, trying to weigh this added complication. Returning to the bed, sits, takes her hand.*

I want to ask you a . . . well it's a kind of private question, okay?

SYLVIA: Harry?

HYMAN: Yes?

>*She draws him to her and kisses him on the mouth.*

SYLVIA: I can't help it.

>*She bursts into tears. He draws her to him and strokes her head.*

HYMAN: Oh God, Sylvia, I'm so sorry . . .

SYLVIA: Help me. Please!

HYMAN: I'm trying to do that, dear.

SYLVIA: I know!

>*He kisses her cheek and releases her. She weeps even more deeply. With a desperate cry filled with her pain she embraces him desperately.*

HYMAN: Oh Sylvia, Sylvia. . . . Here . . .

>*He kisses her forehead and gives her his handkerchief. She wipes her face. He smooths back a strand of her hair.*

SYLVIA: I feel so foolish.

HYMAN: No-no. You're unhappy, dear, not foolish.

SYLVIA: I feel like I'm losing everything, I'm being torn to
    pieces.

HYMAN: I must get someone else here, you must let me!

SYLVIA: Why!—what do you want to know, I'll tell you!

>   *She sobs into her hands. He moves, trying to make
>   a decision . . .*

I trust you, why do I need someone else? What did you
    want to ask me?

HYMAN: —Since this happened to you, have you and Phillip
    had relations?

SYLVIA, *open surprise:* Relations?

HYMAN: He said you did the other night.

SYLVIA: We had *relations* the other night?

HYMAN: But that . . . well he said that by morning you'd
    forgotten. Is that true?

>   *She is motionless, looking past him with immense
>   uncertainty.*

SYLVIA, *alarmed sense of rejection:* Why are you asking me that?

HYMAN: I didn't know what to make of it. . . . I guess I
still don't.

SYLVIA, *deeply embarrassed:* You mean you believe him?

HYMAN: Well . . . I didn't know what to believe.

SYLVIA: Really?

HYMAN: Don't misunderstand me . . .

SYLVIA: You must think I'm crazy, —to forget such a thing.

HYMAN: Oh God no, dear!—I didn't mean anything like
that . . .

SYLVIA: We haven't had relations for over twenty years.

> *The shock pitches him into silence. Now he doesn't
> know what or whom to believe.*

HYMAN: Twenty . . . ? *Breaks off.*

SYLVIA: A few years after Jerome was born.

HYMAN: I just . . . I don't know what to say, Sylvia.

SYLVIA: You never heard of it before with people?

HYMAN: Yes, but not when they're as young as you.

SYLVIA: You might be surprised.

HYMAN: What was it, another woman, or what?

SYLVIA: Oh no.

HYMAN: Then what happened?

SYLVIA: I don't know, I never understood it. He just couldn't anymore.

> *She tries to read his reaction; he doesn't face her directly.*

You believe me, don't you?

HYMAN: Of course I do. But why would he invent a story like that?

SYLVIA, *incredulously:* I can't imagine. There must be something happening to him. How did he come to say that?

HYMAN: It was kind of out of the blue.

SYLVIA: . . . Could he be trying to . . . *Breaks off.*

HYMAN: What.

SYLVIA: . . . Make you think I've gone crazy?

HYMAN: No, you mustn't believe that. I think maybe . . .
you see, he mentioned my so-called reputation with
women, and maybe he was just trying to look . . . I don't
know—competitive. How did this start? Was there some
reason?

SYLVIA: I think I made one mistake. He hadn't come near
me for like—I don't remember anymore—a month
maybe; and . . . I was so young . . . a man to me was so
much stronger that I couldn't imagine I could . . . you
know, hurt him like that.

HYMAN: Like what?

SYLVIA: Well . . . *Small laugh* . . . I was so stupid, I'm still
ashamed of it . . . I mentioned it to my father—who loved
Phillip—and he took him aside and tried to suggest a
doctor. I should never have mentioned it, it was a terrible
mistake, for a while I thought we'd have to have a divorce
. . . it was months before he could say good morning, he
was so furious. *She sighs, shakes her head.* —I don't know,
I guess you just gradually give up and it closes over you
like a grave. But I can't help it, I still pity him; because I
know how it tortures him, it's like a snake eating into his
heart. . . . I mean it's not as though he doesn't like me,
he does, I know it. —Or do you think so?

HYMAN: He says you're his whole life.

She is staring, shaking her head, stunned.

SYLVIA, *with bitter irony:* His whole life! Poor Phillip. —I guess you're right—he was ashamed in front of you, so he made that up.

HYMAN: I want your permission to bring in this man; think about it, I'll call you in the morning.

SYLVIA, *instantly:* Why must you leave? I'm nervous now. Can't you talk to me a few minutes? Come and sit. —Tell me about Germany; you were really there four years?

HYMAN, *sits on the bed:* —The best years of my life.

SYLVIA: And you really made friends with them?

HYMAN: Lots of them. This kind of brutality can't go on much longer, I'm sure of it. You know, German music and literature is some of the greatest in the world; it's impossible for those people to suddenly change into thugs like this. This will all pass, Sylvia, so you ought to have more confidence, you see?—I mean in general, in life, in people. You understand? All this anxiety is unnecessary.

SYLVIA, *sucking up reassurance from him:* I have some yeast cake. I'll make fresh coffee . . .

HYMAN: I'd love to stay but Margaret'll be upset with me.

SYLVIA: Oh. Well call her! Ask her to come over too. *Making to sidle onto her chair.*

HYMAN: No-no . . .

SYLVIA, *a sudden anxiety burst, colored by her feminine disappointment:* For God's sake, why not!

HYMAN: She thinks something's going on with us.

SYLVIA, *pleased surprise—and worriedly:* Oh!

HYMAN: I'll be in touch tomorrow . . .

SYLVIA: Couldn't you just stay till he comes? I'm nervous. Please. Just be here when he comes.

> *Her anxiety forces him back down on the bed. She takes his hand.*

HYMAN: You don't think he'd do something, do you?

SYLVIA: I've never known him so angry. —And I think there's also some trouble with Mr. Case. He can hit, you know. *Shakes her head.* God, everything's so mixed up!

HYMAN: Harriet mentioned something about a steak . . .

SYLVIA, *with a hesitation:* That was nothing. *Pause. Sits there shaking her head, then lifts the newspaper.* But I don't understand—they write that the Germans are starting to pick up Jews right off the street and putting them into . . .

HYMAN, *impatience:* Now Sylvia, I told you . . .

SYLVIA: But you say they were such nice people—how could they change like this!

HYMAN: I don't know! —But . . . here, let me tell you something; after my graduation I spent a two-month vacation in Paris and the French were much more anti-Semitic. Much more. 1927, November and December. In fact, I would say Germany then was probably better than any other country in Europe.

SYLVIA: But that's what I mean, what *happened* to them?

Slight pause.

HYMAN: . . . I'm not understanding you, am I.

She stares at him, becoming transformed.

What are you telling me? Just say what you're thinking right now.

SYLVIA, *struggling:* I . . . I . . .

HYMAN: Don't be frightened, just say it.

SYLVIA, *she has become terrified:* You.

HYMAN: Me! What about me?

SYLVIA: How could you believe I forgot we had relations!

HYMAN: I didn't say I believed it, but I had to ask you since Phillip said it.

SYLVIA: But you believed him a little, didn't you—that I'm crazy . . .

HYMAN, *her persistent intensity unnerving him:* Now stop that! I was only trying to understand what is happening.

SYLVIA: Yes. And what? What is happening?

HYMAN, *forcefully, contained:* . . . Sylvia, dear—what are you trying to tell me?

SYLVIA: Well . . . what . . . *Everything is flying apart for her; she lifts the edge of the newspaper; the focus is clearly far wider than this room. An unbearable anxiety . . .* What is going to become of us?

HYMAN, *indicating the paper:* —But what has Germany got to do with . . . ?

SYLVIA, *shouting; his incomprehension dangerous:* But how can those nice people go out and pick Jews off the street in the middle of a big city like that, and nobody stops them . . . ?

HYMAN, *mystified; he takes her hand, and indicates the newspaper.* I don't understand what that has to do with your condition. What is the connection?

They are close; eyes in contact.

You mean that *I've* changed? Is that it?

SYLVIA, *indicating the newspaper:* I don't know . . . one minute you say you like me and then you turn around and I'm . . .

HYMAN: —Sylvia, I never said you were crazy! Is that it?

SYLVIA: But I think you believed him a little, didn't you?

HYMAN: Listen, I simply must call in somebody . . .

SYLVIA: No! You could help me if you believed me!

HYMAN, *his spine tingling with her fear; a shout:* I do believe you!

SYLVIA: No!—you're not going to put me away somewhere!

HYMAN, *a horrified shout:* Now you stop being ridiculous!

SYLVIA: But . . . but what . . . what . . . *Gripping her head; his uncertainty terrifying her:* What will become of us!

HYMAN, *unnerved:* Now stop it—you are confusing two
things . . . !

SYLVIA: But . . . from now on . . . you mean if a Jew walks
out of his house, do they arrest him . . . ?

HYMAN: I'm telling you this won't last.

SYLVIA, *with a weird, blind, violent persistence:* But what do
they do with them?

HYMAN: I don't know! I'm sorry, I have to go. *Makes to
leave.*

SYLVIA: Why!!

HYMAN: I'm out of my depth! I can't help you! *He strides to
the periphery.*

SYLVIA: But why don't they run out of the country!

> *The passionate incongruity stops him.*

Why are they staying there! What is the matter with those
people! Don't you understand . . . ? *Screaming:* . . . This
is an *emergency! She flings off the blanket and is suddenly on
her feet.* They are beating up little children! What if they
kill those children!

> *She is striding around, yelling at him; he stands there
> amazed.*

Why do they stay there, what's the matter with those people! What are they waiting for! Where is Roosevelt! Where is England! Somebody should do something before they murder us all!

> *Hyman is staring in astonishment. She looks down at her legs and sways, starts to faint. He catches her and pulls her to the bed and lays her down, and lightly slaps her cheeks . . .*

HYMAN: Sylvia? Sylvia!

> *Phillip enters.*

Run cold water on a towel!

PHILLIP: What happened!

HYMAN: Do it, goddam you!

> *Phillip rushes out.*

Sylvia!—oh good, that's it, keep looking at me, that's it dear, keep your eyes open . . .

> *Phillip hurries in with a towel and gives it to Hyman, who presses it onto her forehead and back of her neck.*

There we are, that's better, how do you feel? Can you speak? You want to sit up? Come.

*He helps her to sit up. She looks around and then
at Phillip.*

SYLVIA: Oh. Hello.

GELLBURG, *to Hyman:* Did *she* call *you?*

HYMAN, *hesitates; and in an angry tone* . . . Well no, to tell
the truth.

GELLBURG: Then what are you doing here?

HYMAN: I stopped by, I was worried about her.

GELLBURG: You were worried about her. Why were you
worried about her?

HYMAN, *anger is suddenly sweeping him:* Because she is desperate to be loved.

GELLBURG, *off guard, astonished:* You don't say!

HYMAN: Yes, I do say. *To her:* I want you to try to move
your legs. Try it, dear.

She tries; nothing happens.

I'll be at home if you need me; don't be afraid to call
anytime. We'll talk about this more tomorrow. Good
night.

SYLVIA, *faintly, afraid:* Good night.

> *With a quick, outraged glance at Gellburg, Hyman leaves.*

GELLBURG, *reaching for his authority:* That's some attitude he's got, ordering me around like that. I'm going to see about getting somebody else tomorrow. *He sits and removes his shoes.* Jersey seems to get further and further away, I'm exhausted.

SYLVIA: I just stood up and started walking.

GELLBURG: What are you talking about?

SYLVIA: For a minute. I don't know what happened, my strength suddenly came back.

GELLBURG: I knew it! I told you you could! Try it again, come.

SYLVIA, *she tries to raise her legs.* I can't now.

GELLBURG: Why not! Come, this is wonderful . . . ! *Reaches for her.*

SYLVIA: Phillip, listen . . . I don't want to change, I want Hyman.

GELLBURG, *his purse-mouthed grin:* What's so good about him?—you're still laying there, practically dead to the world.

SYLVIA: He helped me get up, I don't know why. I feel he can get me walking again.

GELLBURG: Why does it have to be him?

SYLVIA: Because I can talk to him! I want *him. An outburst:* And I don't want to discuss it again!

GELLBURG: Well we'll see.

SYLVIA: We will not see!

GELLBURG: What's this tone of voice?

SYLVIA, *trembling out of control:* It's a Jewish woman's tone of voice!

GELLBURG: A Jewish woman . . . ! What are you talking about, are you crazy?

SYLVIA: Don't you call me crazy, Phillip! I'm talking about it! They are smashing windows and beating children! I am talking about it! *Screams at him:* I am talking about it, Phillip!

> *She grips her head in her confusion. He is stock still; horrified, fearful.*

GELLBURG: What . . . "beating children"?

SYLVIA: Never mind. Don't sleep with me again.

GELLBURG: How can you say that to me?

SYLVIA: I can't bear it. You give me terrible dreams. I'm sorry, Phillip. Maybe in a while but not now.

GELLBURG, *comes to the bed, goes to his knees clasping his hands together:* Sylvia, you will kill me if we can't be together . . .

SYLVIA: You told him we had relations?

GELLBURG, *beginning to weep:* Don't, Sylvia . . . !

SYLVIA: You little liar!—you want him to think I'm crazy? Is that it? *Now she breaks into weeping.*

GELLBURG: No! It just . . . it came out, I didn't know what I was saying!

SYLVIA: *That I forgot we had relations?! Phillip?*

GELLBURG: Stop that! Don't say anymore.

SYLVIA: I'm going to say anything I want to.

GELLBURG, *weeping:* You will kill me . . . !

They are silent for a moment.

SYLVIA: What I did with my life! Out of ignorance. Out of not wanting to shame you in front of other people. A whole life. Gave it away like a couple of pennies—I took better care of my shoes. *Turns to him.* —You want to talk to me about it now? Take me seriously, Phillip. What happened? I know it's all you ever thought about, isn't that true? *What happened?* Just so I'll know.

A long pause.

GELLBURG: I'm ashamed to mention it. It's ridiculous.

SYLVIA: What are you talking about?

GELLBURG: It was a mistake. But I was ignorant, I couldn't help myself. —When you said you wanted to go back to the firm.

SYLVIA: What are you talking about?—when?

GELLBURG: When you had Jerome . . . and suddenly you didn't want to keep the house anymore.

SYLVIA: And? —You didn't want me to go back to business, so I didn't.

He doesn't speak; her rage an inch below.

Well what? I didn't, did I?

GELLBURG: You held it against me, having to stay home, you know you did. You've probably forgotten, but not a day passed, not a person could come into this house that you didn't keep saying how wonderful and interesting it used to be for you in business. You never forgave me, Sylvia.

She evades his gaze.

So whenever I . . . when I started to touch you, I felt that.

SYLVIA: You felt what?

GELLBURG: That you didn't want me to be the man here. And then, on top of that when you didn't want any more children . . . everything inside me just dried up. And maybe it was also that to me it was a miracle you ever married me in the first place.

SYLVIA: You mean your face?

He turns slightly.

What have you got against your face? A Jew can have a Jewish face.

Pause.

GELLBURG: I can't help my thoughts, nobody can. . . . I admit it was a mistake, I tried a hundred times to talk to

you, but I couldn't. I kept waiting for myself to change.
Or you. And then we got to where it didn't seem to
matter anymore. So I left it that way. And I couldn't
change anything anymore.

Pause.

SYLVIA: This is a whole life we're talking about.

GELLBURG: But couldn't we . . . if I taught you to drive
and you could go anywhere you liked. . . . Or maybe
you could find a position you liked . . . ?

She is staring ahead.

We have to sleep together.

SYLVIA: No.

GELLBURG: How can this be?

She is motionless.

Sylvia? *Pause.* Do you want to kill me?

*She is staring ahead, he is watching and awaiting
her reply. He shouts.*

Is that it!

She turns to him, but says nothing.

Blackout.

Gellburg is seated in Mr. Case's office. He is steeling himself, swallowing, making little coughs to clear his throat. His skin is yellowish, his eyes stark, he keeps trying to breathe deeply.

Case enters. His manner is formal and cold. He stands before Gellburg, who has gotten to his feet.

CASE: Good morning, Gellburg.

GELLBURG: Good morning, Mr. Case.

CASE: I understand you wish to see me.

GELLBURG: There was just something I felt I should say.

CASE: Certainly. *He goes to a chair and sits.* Yes?

GELLBURG: It's just that I would never in this world do anything against you or Brooklyn Guarantee. I don't have to tell you, it's the only place I've ever worked in my life. My whole life is here. I'm more proud of this company than almost anything except my own son. What I'm trying to say is that this whole business with Wanamaker's was only because I didn't want to leave a stone unturned. Two or three years from now I didn't want to wake up one morning and Wanamaker's is gone and there you are paying New York taxes on a building in the middle of a dying neighborhood.

Case lets him hang there. He begins getting flustered.

Frankly, I don't even remember what this whole thing was about. I feel I've lost some of your confidence, and it's . . . well, it's unfair, I feel.

CASE: I understand.

GELLBURG, *he waits, but that's it.* But . . . but don't you believe me?

CASE: I think I do.

GELLBURG: But . . . you seem to be . . . you don't seem . . .

CASE: The fact remains that I've lost the building.

GELLBURG: But are you . . . I mean you're not still thinking that I had something going on with Allan Kershowitz, are you?

CASE: Put it this way—I hope as time goes on that my old confidence will return. That's about as far as I can go, and I don't think you can blame me, can you. *He stands.*

GELLBURG, *despite himself his voice rises:* But how can I work if you're this way? I mean you have to trust a man, don't you?

CASE, *begins to indicate he must leave:* I'll have to ask you to . . .

GELLBURG, *shouting:* I don't deserve this! You can't do this to me! It's not fair, Mr. Case, I had nothing to do with Allan Kershowitz! I hardly know the man! And the little I do know I don't even like him, I'd certainly never get into a deal with him, for God's sake! *Exploding:* This is . . . this whole thing is . . . I don't understand it, what is happening, what the hell is happening, what have I got to do with Allan Kershowitz, just because he's also a Jew?

CASE, *incredulously and angering:* What? What on earth are you talking about!

GELLBURG: Excuse me. I didn't mean that.

CASE: I don't understand . . . how could you say a thing like that!

GELLBURG: Please. I don't feel well, excuse me . . .

CASE, *his resentment mounting:* But how could you say such a thing! It's an outrage, Gellburg!

Gellburg takes a step to leave and goes to his knees, his head hanging between his arms as he tries to breathe. Case hurries to him.

CASE: What is it? Gellburg? *He springs up and goes to the periphery.* Call an ambulance! Hurry, for God's sake! *He rushes out, shouting:* Quick, get a doctor! It's Gellburg! Gellburg has collapsed!

Gellburg remains on his hands and knees trying to keep from falling over, gasping.

Blackout

SCENE SIX

The cellist plays, the music falls away.

Gellburg's bedroom. He is in bed. An oxygen tank stands nearby. Hyman is listening to his heart. Now he puts his stethoscope back into his bag, and sits on a chair beside the bed.

HYMAN: I'll have to say it again, —you belong in the hospital, you must go back.

GELLBURG: I can't stand it there, it smells like a zoo; and to lay in a bed where some stranger died . . . I hate it. If I'm going out I'll go from here.

HYMAN: I'm trying to help you.

GELLBURG: I appreciate that. —And I don't want to leave Sylvia.

HYMAN: Well . . . the nurse should be here around six.

GELLBURG: I'm wondering if I need her—I think the pain is practically gone.

HYMAN: Let her watch you overnight. I'm heading back to my office now.

GELLBURG: . . . I'd love to talk to you. . . . But I don't want to hold you up.

HYMAN: I've got a minute, what is it?

GELLBURG: I'm choking on my thoughts. *He doesn't continue.*

HYMAN: What is it?

GELLBURG, *struggling with embarrassment:* I can't . . . I can't get to the bottom of myself. I thought I would last longer—that there'd be time to think about things.

HYMAN: You might have years, nobody can predict.

GELLBURG: I can't keep my thoughts straight. *A short embarrassed self-deprecating laugh.* It's unbelievable—I don't have a job anymore. I just can't believe it.

HYMAN: You sure? It didn't sound that bad from what you told me. Maybe you can clear it up with your boss when you go back.

GELLBURG: How can I go back? He made a fool of me. It's infuriating.

HYMAN: What happened, exactly?

GELLBURG: I'm too tired to go into it now. I tell you—I never wanted to see it this way but he goes sailing around on the ocean and meanwhile I'm foreclosing Brooklyn for them. That's what it boils down to. You got some lousy rotten job to do, get Gellburg, send in the Yid. Close down a business, throw somebody out of his home. . . . And now to accuse me . . .

HYMAN: But is all this news to you? That's the system, isn't it?

GELLBURG: But to accuse me of double-crossing the *company*! That is absolutely unfair . . . it was like a hammer between the eyes. And would he ever *dare* make such an accusation to one of his own?—I don't think so! I mean to me Brooklyn Guarantee—for God's sake, Brooklyn Guarantee was like . . . like . . .

HYMAN: You're getting too excited, Phillip . . . come on now. *Changing the subject:* —I understand your son is coming back from the Philippines.

GELLBURG, *he catches his breath for a moment.* . . . She show you his telegram? He's trying to make it here by Monday. *Scared eyes and a grin.* Or will I last till Monday?

HYMAN: You've got to start thinking about more positive things—seriously, your system needs a rest. I'll stop by later . . .

GELLBURG, *looks toward the floor.* Who's that talking?

HYMAN: Sounds like the radio downstairs.

GELLBURG: She's scaring herself to death with the news.

HYMAN: I'll call later.

GELLBURG: . . . I wish I could ask you about something but
   I . . . it's hard for me. *A smiling head shake at his incapacity.*
   —Can you spare five minutes?

HYMAN, *sitting:* What do you want to say, Phillip?

GELLBURG, *almost holding his breath:* The thing she's so afraid
   of . . . is me, isn't it.

HYMAN: Well . . . among other things.

GELLBURG, *shock:* It's me?

HYMAN: I think so . . . partly.

GELLBURG, *shaking his head, tears in his eyes:* But why?

HYMAN: You'd know that better than I, Phillip.

GELLBURG: But she talks to you.

HYMAN: Yes, but about her feelings, not about you, particularly.

GELLBURG: She's faking this, isn't she.

HYMAN: That's impossible. Why do you go on repeating it?

GELLBURG: It's to get back at me. I know it.

Hyman is silent.

It is, isn't it? Well, tell me!

HYMAN, *takes a moment to answer:* If it is, she's not doing it consciously.

GELLBURG, *a growing intensity:* But why? For what? Does she say?

HYMAN: You've lived with her, you'd know that better than I . . .

GELLBURG: But you have no *idea*?

HYMAN: I said the first time we talked, remember? I don't think people get sick alone; you're part of this, Phillip; you've got to start looking into yourself before you try figuring her. I'm not criticizing you.

Pause. Gellburg's manner has hardened.

I'd like to arrange for the ambulance, okay?

GELLBURG: Did you do it with her?

HYMAN, *shocked outrage and guilt:* Did I *do* it with her! What the hell are you talking about? What is the matter with you! It's ridiculous!

GELLBURG: I see how she looks at you! —You didn't answer me.

HYMAN: No. Is that good enough?

> *Gellburg presses his fingers against his eyes to regain control.*

Of course if she did do something it'd be hard to blame her, wouldn't it.

GELLBURG: It would? Why?

HYMAN: Never mind. Can I arrange the ambulance . . . ?

GELLBURG, *welling up:* How could she be frightened of me! I worship her! *Quickly controlling:* Please, stay a minute. How could everything turn out to be the opposite—I made my son in this bed and now I'm dying in it . . . *Breaks off, downing a cry.* My thoughts keep flying around—everything from years ago keeps coming back like it was last week. Like the day we bought this bed. Abraham & Straus. It was so sunny and beautiful. I took the whole day off. (God, it's almost thirty years ago!) . . . Then we had a soda at Schrafft's—of course they don't hire Jews but the chocolate ice cream is the best. Then we went over to Orchard Street for bargains. Bought our first pots and sheets, blankets, pillowcases. The street was full of pushcarts and men with long beards like a hundred years ago. It's funny . . . *Half-condescendingly:* I felt so at home and happy there that day, a street full of Jews, one Moses after another. *Pause; he is caught up; smiles now.* . . . But they all turned to watch her go by, those fakers. She was a knockout; sometimes walking down a street I couldn't believe I was married to her. Listen . . . *Breaks off, with some diffidence:* You're an educated man, I only went to high school—I wish we could talk about the Jews.

HYMAN: I never studied the history, if that's what you . . .

GELLBURG: . . . I don't know where I am . . .

HYMAN: You mean as a Jew?

GELLBURG: Do you think about it much? Because I would never know you were Jewish except for your name. I never . . . for instance, a Jew in love with horses is something I never heard of.

HYMAN: My grandfather in Odessa was a horse dealer.

GELLBURG: You don't say!

HYMAN: I have cousins up near Syracuse who're still in the business—they break horses. You know there are Chinese Jews.

GELLBURG: I heard of that! And they look Chinese?

HYMAN: They are Chinese. They'd probably say you don't look Jewish.

GELLBURG: Ha! That's funny. *His small laugh disappears; he stares.* Why is it so hard to be a Jew?

HYMAN: It's hard to be anything.

GELLBURG: No, it's different for them. Being a Jew is a full-time job. Except you don't think about it much, do you. —Like when you're on your horse, or . . .

HYMAN: It's not an obsession for me . . .

GELLBURG: But why did you . . . ? Maybe it's too personal . . .

HYMAN: Go ahead.

GELLBURG: How'd you come to marry a shiksa?

HYMAN, *uncomfortably:* We were thrown together when I was interning, and we got very close, and . . . well she was a good partner, she helped me, and still does. And I loved her.

GELLBURG: . . . I'm only trying to figure it out—a Jewish woman couldn't help you?

HYMAN: Sure. But it just didn't happen. —I've got to get back . . . *Stands to go.*

GELLBURG: It wasn't so you wouldn't seem Jewish. (?)

HYMAN, *coldly:* I never pretended I wasn't Jewish.

GELLBURG, *almost shaking with some fear:* Look, don't be mad, I'm only trying to figure out . . .

HYMAN, *sensing the underlying hostility:* What are you driving at, I don't understand this whole conversation.

GELLBURG, *his anxiety blooming on his face:* I don't know how to tell you. —You see, I was never scared in my life.

HYMAN: What are you talking about . . . ?

GELLBURG, *his body quakes; crying out:* Hyman . . . Help me! *Ashamed of his outburst he covers his face. His hands are shaking.*

HYMAN, *his physicianship surging, he comforts:* All right, let's take it easy. *Tries to lower Gellburg's hands.* Come on now.

> *Gellburg lets him draw his hands down.*

I'll send over something to put you to sleep, okay? —What is it? What's frightening you?

GELLBURG: It doesn't bother you—what's happening?

HYMAN, *a stab:* —You talking about the Germans?

GELLBURG: The . . . the whole thing.

HYMAN: What whole thing?

GELLBURG: Just . . . just . . . *He lifts his hands, palms up, looking around as though at life, the world* . . . The whole thing. —I'll tell you . . . many times I had to go into some terrible neighborhoods; you know, mortgages, unpaid rents. Run into a lot of characters you wouldn't want to meet in the dark. Never bothered me. That was the job and I did it . . .

HYMAN: What can I tell you? The world is frightening.

GELLBURG, *quietly, from the center of his soul:* Hyman.

HYMAN: Yes.

GELLBURG, *overriding embarrassment:* I want my wife back.

HYMAN, *helplessly:* Yes. Well what can I say, maybe as time goes on you'll both . . .

GELLBURG: I want her back before something happens. I feel like there's nothing inside me, I feel empty. I want her back.

HYMAN: Phillip, what can I do about that?

GELLBURG: Never mind . . . Since you started coming around . . . in those boots . . . like some kind of *horseback rider* . . . ?

HYMAN, *alarmed:* What the hell are you talking about! *He starts to leave.*

GELLBURG: . . . You're a Jew! Why are you posing? Since you came around she looks down at me like a miserable piece of shit!

HYMAN: Phillip . . .

GELLBURG: Don't "Phillip" me, just stop it!

HYMAN: Don't scream at me, Phillip, you know how to get your wife back!

Gellburg slowly lies back on the pillow.

Long pause.

GELLBURG: So I did this to her.

HYMAN: I'm sure you didn't mean to. It's also what's going on in Europe.

GELLBURG: What do I have to do with that?

HYMAN: I really don't understand it. I think there's some connection in her mind.

GELLBURG: She actually told you that I . . . ? *Breaks off.*

HYMAN: It came out while we were talking. It was bound to, sooner or later, wasn't it?

GELLBURG: Tell me what she said.

HYMAN: That there hadn't been relations for a long time. Twenty years.

Pause.

GELLBURG: What can I do?

HYMAN: I don't really know. When you're feeling better, maybe sit down and try to talk, both of you.

GELLBURG: —Something sticks in my mind that I've always wanted to talk to somebody about. It's like it happened this morning. But years ago, . . . when I used to do it with her, I would feel almost like a small baby on top of her, like she was giving me birth. In bed next to me she was like a . . . a marble god. That's some idea, heh? I worshiped her, Hyman, from the day I laid eyes on her.

HYMAN: I'm sorry for you, Phillip. —I'll leave you now.

GELLBURG: If I get better I would like to try again. You think she would?

HYMAN: I can't answer. —It's not only a question of sex, you understand.

GELLBURG: You know what I think? I wonder maybe if I'd worked for a Jewish firm . . . I think it twisted me all around.

HYMAN: You can't live in a ghetto.

GELLBURG: That's it, you see; I wanted to be an American like everybody else . . . and now I don't know where I am. —But you don't even think we're different, do you.

HYMAN: I think everybody's different.

GELLBURG: . . . You believe in God? No, huh?

HYMAN: I'm a socialist. I think we're at the end of religion.

GELLBURG: You mean everybody working for the government.

HYMAN: It's the only future that makes any rational sense.

GELLBURG: God forbid. But how can there be Jews if there's no God?

HYMAN: Oh, they'll find something to worship. The Christians will too—maybe different brands of ketchup.

GELLBURG, *laughs*. Boy, the things you come out with sometimes . . . !

HYMAN: —Some day we're all going to look like a lot of
monkeys running around trying to figure out a coconut.
I have to get back.

GELLBURG: Hyman . . .

HYMAN: I have to go, Phillip.

GELLBURG: —I think the pain is coming again.

HYMAN: Be quiet. *Takes out his stethoscope, places it on Gellburg's chest.*

GELLBURG: She believes in you, Hyman . . .

HYMAN: Sssh.

GELLBURG: . . . I want you to tell her—tell her I'm going
to change. She has no right to be so frightened. Of me
or anything else. They will never destroy us. When the
last Jew dies, the light of the world will go out. She has
to understand that—those Germans are shooting at
the sun!

HYMAN: Be quiet.

GELLBURG: She is faking this paralysis. Is she trying to destroy me . . . ?

HYMAN: Be quiet.

GELLBURG: . . . And you sit there with her . . . *His chest heaving*.

HYMAN: I haven't touched her. Just stop it. *He feels his pulse*.

GELLBURG: How can she be so afraid of me? Tell me the truth.

HYMAN: I don't know; maybe, for one thing—these remarks you're always making about Jews.

GELLBURG: What remarks?

HYMAN: Like not wanting to be mistaken for Goldberg.

GELLBURG: So I'm a Nazi?

HYMAN: Who said you're a Nazi?

GELLBURG: Well is Gellburg Goldberg? It's not, is it?

HYMAN: No, but continually making the point is kind of . . .

GELLBURG: Kind of what?

HYMAN: Well, it . . . *Breaks off*. I don't know what to tell you.

GELLBURG, *a wild, victorious smile:* Because you're not telling the truth—

HYMAN: Stop calling me a liar, you're totally confused . . . !

GELLBURG: I know what she's doing, and I forbid you to blame me for her, goddam you!

HYMAN, *outraged:* Stop calling me names, will you?

GELLBURG: What are you hiding from me?

HYMAN: All right, you want the truth? Do you? Look in the mirror sometime!

GELLBURG: . . . In the mirror!

HYMAN: You hate yourself, that's what's scaring her to death. That's my opinion. How it's possible I don't know, but I think you helped paralyze her with this "Jew, Jew, Jew" coming out of your mouth and the same time she reads it in the paper and it's coming out of the radio day and night? You wanted to know what I think . . . that's what I think. *He picks up his bag.*

GELLBURG: Don't go 'way! Please, Harry, I'll explode here by myself! *He hurries, pursued . . .* —I tell you there are some days I feel like going and sitting in the *schul* with the old men and pulling the *talles* over my head and be a full-time Jew the rest of my life. With the sidelocks and the black hat, and settle it once and for all. Yes. And other times . . . yes, I could almost kill them. They infuriate me. I am ashamed of them and that I look like them. *Gasping again:* —Why must we be different? Why is it? What is it for?

HYMAN: And supposing it turns out that we're *not* different, who are you going to blame then?

GELLBURG: What are you talking about?

HYMAN: I'm talking about all this grinding and screaming that's going on inside you—you're wearing yourself out for nothing, Phillip, absolutely nothing! —I'll tell you a secret—I have all kinds coming into my office, and there's not one of them who one way or another is not persecuted. Yes. *Everybody's* persecuted. The poor by the rich, the rich by the poor, the black by the white, the white by the black, the men by the women, the women by the men, the Catholics by the Protestants, the Protestants by the Catholics—and of course all of them by the Jews. I even wonder sometimes if maybe that's what holds the country together! It's really amazing—you can't find anybody who's persecuting anybody else.

GELLBURG: So you mean like . . . there's no Hitler?

HYMAN: Hitler? Hitler is the perfect example of the persecuted man! I've heard him—he kvetches like an elephant was standing on his pecker! He's turned his whole beautiful country into one gigantic kvetch!

GELLBURG: So what's the solution?

HYMAN: I don't see any. Except the mirror. But nobody's going to look at himself and ask what *he's* doing—you might as well tell him to take a seat in the hottest part of hell. —I'll arrange for the ambulance.

GELLBURG, *his breathing is now coming in gasps:* What did I do? —I worshiped her . . . *A deep gasp.*

HYMAN: Ssh! *Hyman hurriedly takes a pill out of a bottle and forces it under his tongue.*

GELLBURG: We're different, Hyman—you're wrong . . .

HYMAN: Be quiet!

GELLBURG: I'm a Jew! And they will never destroy us!

HYMAN: Okay, be quiet!

GELLBURG: If anybody ever laid a hand on Sylvia . . . I would kill the whole world. If she is ever touched I . . .

HYMAN: Don't talk, stop it . . .

GELLBURG, *defiantly:* You're wrong, Hyman, we are here forever! Forever!

HYMAN: Stop it!

GELLBURG: Please God let me see my Jerome. —I want to see the first Jewish general in the Army of the United States!

> *Sylvia enters in wheelchair. He looks at her wide-eyed.*

So! You walk up the stairs?

SYLVIA, *to Hyman:* He looks terrible!—can't you do something?

GELLBURG: How do you walk up the stairs!

SYLVIA: You've seen me upstairs half a dozen times, Flora carries me up on her back.

GELLBURG: That stick carries you? What am I, an idiot?

SYLVIA: She's strong as an ox. How is he?

HYMAN: I can't be responsible if he doesn't go to a hospital.

SYLVIA: You hear him?

GELLBURG: Don't forget, I put a hundred-dollar deposit on the Dodge. But if you don't want it it's returnable.

SYLVIA: What do I care about the Dodge! *To Hyman:* Go downstairs and call an ambulance.

Hyman starts out.

GELLBURG: Hyman! I only ask one thing—don't do it in this house.

SYLVIA: *What!*

GELLBURG: It's all right, you can get up now.

SYLVIA: Get up? What do you mean, get up? I can't get up!

GELLBURG: It's all right, my Sylvia. Come, stand up. I deserve it.

SYLVIA: What is he talking about?

GELLBURG: You don't have to do this anymore. I would never harm you, Sylvia.

SYLVIA, *to Hyman:* I don't understand what he's . . .

GELLBURG: Tell me you don't believe such a thing.

SYLVIA: Believe what? What are you talking about?

GELLBURG: Sometimes you look at me so frightened. Like I would harm you.

SYLVIA: I said you would harm me?

GELLBURG: The way you look sometimes.

SYLVIA, *at a complete loss:* Why would you harm me? What does that mean?

GELLBURG: I can't bear it, Sylvia, it's a knife in my heart to see you like this . . . *He throws off the cover and gets out of bed.*

HYMAN, *trying to detain him:* You mustn't, Phillip, get back . . .

GELLBURG: . . . Stand on your feet, Sylvia.

> *She looks up at him amazed, bewildered. He is weakly trying to draw her up by the arm.*

Please, get up, get up . . .

SYLVIA, *trying to undo his grip:* I can't, Phillip!

> *Hyman is trying to pull him away.*

HYMAN: You must get back in bed!

GELLBURG, *pulling on her arm:* You don't have to do this anymore, Sylvia! I can't bear it, get up!

HYMAN, *pulling him away by force:* Stop this . . . !

GELLBURG: This is a knife . . . !

He collapses on the floor. Hyman immediately starts pumping on his chest. Now he tries to reach with one hand for the oxygen mask hanging from the tank while continuing to pump with the other, but it is beyond his grasp.

HYMAN: Call the maid to get me the mask!

Sylvia leans forward in the wheelchair, and with enormous effort raises herself to her feet; she is out of Hyman's line of sight and takes the steps to the mask and hands it to him over his shoulder.

SYLVIA, *in almost a whisper:* Oh, Phillip, Phillip!

Seeing the mask, Hyman turns with a quick shocked glance at her, takes the mask from her, and places it on Gellburg's face. She turns the tank valve, opening the flow. With his free hand he takes a needle out of his bag and plunges it into Gellburg's chest. Then takes out his stethoscope and listens.

SYLVIA: Oh Phillip. Oh Phillip. Oh Phillip . . .

A long moment. Still standing, she continues whispering her incantation.

HYMAN, *coming away from Gellburg:* I'll call my wife to get the ambulance.

Her arms are raised up as she looks down in amazement at her legs. As he leaves . . .

Do you have some feeling?

SYLVIA:

She feels her thighs.

It came back!

HYMAN, *joyously, awestruck:* My God!

He hurries out. She slowly walks to Gellburg.

SYLVIA: Oh Phillip, please . . . look at me . . . please . . .

A subliminal awareness of guilt, remote and uncertain, charges her voice.

Phillip, I'm walking! Please, try to open your eyes. Please, look at me, dear —I'm standing up!

Between laughter and immense mourning . . . a pleading shout.

Can you hear me?

She takes his limp hand and kisses it desperately.

Phillip, please . . . please . . . !

*Hyman enters, goes quickly to Gellburg; she moves
aside as he feels his pulse, places a stethoscope to his
chest. She presses her hands against her thighs as
though they were not hers.*

What happened to me?

Hyman looks up to her.

Do you know?

HYMAN, *a hesitation; a decision; then a tone of immense forbear-
ance . . . :* No.

SYLVIA: Will he live?

HYMAN: I don't know yet. But you . . . you'll be strong
now, won't you. —I have to tell you, it's wonderful to
see you standing up, straight and fine. You see how strong
you really are? So you won't be afraid anymore, will you.

*She has turned toward Gellburg; he sees the guilt in
her eyes.*

You mustn't blame yourself, dear—the world is too terrible; I think you just . . . didn't want to go under. And
somehow . . .

She turns back to him.

you haven't.

SYLVIA: It was you; I have you to thank, Harry.

HYMAN: The sight of you standing there now I'll remember as long as I live.

Sylvia raises her hand and almost touches his face. Margaret enters and she lowers her hand.

MARGARET: The ambulance is coming.

Margaret starts to look at Gellburg on the bed when she realizes and looks down at Sylvia's legs, and with great surprise . . .

What happened!

SYLVIA, *with a half-shrug, lifting her hands:* I don't know!

She moves to Gellburg, as Margaret turns to Hyman for explanation.

HYMAN: She just . . . suddenly stood up!

MARGARET, *with a certain overly emphatic exhilaration almost verging on a left-out tone:* How wonderful!

SYLVIA:

She lifts Gellburg's hand and kisses it, and with an outpouring of a grief that is half guilty and half hope-driven . . .

Phillip? Please, I want you to look at me.

Releasing his hand, she grips her head.

Please! Please . . . please, Phillip, look at me . . .

Crying out, unable to hold back her victory.

I'm all right! Can you hear me? I'm all right, Phillip! Can you hear me!

The three stand waiting, as though for a sound of their release.

THE END.